# T H E
# H O R S E
# HUNTERS

| | |
|---|---|
| *A Day No Pigs Would Die* | *Hub* |
| *Path of Hunters* | *Mr. Little* |
| *Millie's Boy* | *Clunie* |
| *Soup (a series)* | *Justice Lion* |
| *Fawn* | *Kirk's Law* |
| *Wild Cat* | *Banjo* |
| *Hamilton* | *Fiction is Folks* |
| *Hang for Treason* | *The Seminole Seed* |
| *Rabbits and Redcoats* | *Dukes* |
| *King of Kazoo (a musical)* | *Spanish Hoof* |
| *Trig (a series)* | *Jo Silver* |
| *Last Sunday* | *Secrets of Successful Fiction* |
| *The King's Iron* | *My Vermont* |
| *Patooie* | *My Vermont II* |
| *Eagle Fur* | *Hallapoosa* |
| *Basket Case* | *Arly* |

# T H E
# HORSE
# HUNTERS

Robert Newton Peck

RANDOM HOUSE
NEW YORK

F
Pec

Library of Congress Cataloging-in-Publication Data

Peck, Robert Newton.
The horse hunters.

Summary: In 1932 in Florida, despite his older
brother's objections, fifteen-year-old Ladd finds
himself, through a series of unforeseen circumstances,
traveling alone more than 100 miles to bring back
wild horses for the rodeo and for breeding.
[1. Horses—Fiction.   2. Brothers—Fiction.
3. Florida—Fiction]   I. Title.
PZ7.P339Ho   1988       [Fic]          88-42659
ISBN 0-394-56980-6

Manufactured in the United States of America
24689753
First Edition

Book design by Debbie Glasserman

*The Horse Hunters* . . . is dedicated to a few gentle people
who believe that horses are worth knowing:

Tobin Corbett
Mex Cruz
Betty Old Rabbit
Rigger Swicegood
Hank Redpath

Plus a thank-you to Camille and Jim Flankey
and to Mary Acre,
who know far more than I do about carousels.

Robert Newton Peck
Longwood, Florida
1988

# T H E
# H O R S E
# HUNTERS

# PROLOGUE

## 1905

HE KICKED VICIOUSLY.

The foal was resisting his birth.

Inside the wild mare's belly it was silent and dark, and the wet warmth cradled him, rocking him gently with the frequent movements of her body. But now her contractions were pressuring him to be born. Again he kicked his dam.

Lying on the sandy Florida flats, hidden from the other mares and the red stallion, the mustang mare withstood the violent surgings of her labor, straining to rid herself of this obstinate colt.

Above, a tropical sky had deepened to purple while the hurricane roared across the peninsula, uprooting trees as it came. Salty air freckled with leaves, sand, and bits of branches. The mare's strong body convulsed. Around her, rabbits and squirrels and birds darted for cover, bolting from the whipping storm. A hawk screamed at the wind for driving his prey underground. With the harsh pelting rain came silver cracks of lightning, splitting a brittle sky into inky shards and fragments, followed by a deafening wrath of thunder.

The mare did not panic. Eyes protruding, she grunted harder, confining her foal into the birth canal.

Inside, the colt moved helplessly now, his delicate front hoofs stretching before him, beneath his muzzle, as he felt the maternal pressure increasing on all flanks, crushing his will to remain in warmth and safety. Swiftly he became part of an explosion, a missile, a deliverance of living tissue from his dam, as he was expelled onto the soaking Florida earth with brutal force. There was no air, little light, until the wild mare's teeth tore at the membrane that enclosed him.

Her jaws snapped the life cord.

He was free.

Gasping his first breath, he squinted to protect his eyes from an onslaught of hurtling debris, aware that his mother's tongue was licking him, nudging, encouraging him to survive in this raging violence of wind and biting rain. Bleating, he tried to sit up, then failed, falling back to ground water and damp unwelcoming mud. To the foal, during these early moments of life in the open, the noise and blinding flashes were intolerable, so again he cried out in a confusion of fear and discomfort. But the dam's tongue caressed his face, eyes, ears, commanding him to gain his feet, as she had regained hers.

Her unshod hoof pawed at him, gently, yet with a singular purpose, to spur his determination.

The colt was pure white.

His pelt seemed so inconsistent with the outback's green and brown, as though foreign, a ghostlike alien foal. Yet he struggled to find his footing, delicate legs wobbling, fighting his weakness to stagger beneath her where there was shelter. And one thing more. The swollen hot teat of her udder, which he began to suck with a fury until his mouth and gullet were flooding with pleasure. Gulping, he allowed the warming nourishment to invade his belly, fortifying him with every desperate swallow.

He fell, but rose again.

In minutes, he could stand and walk and soon trot along by her side, following this comforting source of milk and shelter. Head high, her nostrils flaring, the mare searched a fierce wind, fearing that the band of horses might be moving. The dominant red stallion who had bred her and sired this foal, as well as all others, would be demanding that she and her still-trembling newborn travel with the band. The foal must run or die.

Her trot extended, stretching into a long loping canter, but the white colt kept pace with her, keeping up, appearing to strengthen in body and spirit with every stride. In less than an hour following his birth he could gallop through the storm with almost the stallion's speed.

A YEAR PASSED.

The white colt was far from a foal. As his chest expanded, his coat thickened, and he began to grow more teeth than his dam.

Before two years he had surpassed her size. The red stallion, however, had begun to persecute him, driving him away from the band with kicks and bites. Yet the white two-year-old shadowed them from a safe distance, watching the stallion defend his foals and females from bears and panthers. Always he could smell the mares, tasting the yet-unknown fragrance with his nostrils, a scent that would silently bugle him to his destiny.

But it was the stallion who fascinated him. The great red, who always bore fresh-bleeding wounds, as well as scars of earlier battles. Time and again, the young white horse saw his sire beating a challenger to death with those striking front hoofs hitting like hammers. Day upon day, at a distance he studied his sire, watching him mount his mares, the hairs of mane and tail erect as though possessing a desiring fury of their own.

Observing, the white colt reared, boxing the sky with his hoofs, shaking his handsome young head in intemperate ecstasy.

Then, his body quivering, he would call to the band from afar, nickering a lonely cry of longing, pleading, desperate to return.

Long ago, he had outgrown the mare's milk, once he had lowered his muzzle to his first taste of fresh Florida grass. With every breath of cooling night air, his lungs filled and pumped as he galloped, always alone, in long distance-devouring strides that seemed to float his powerful white body above four sturdy legs. He was male. He felt male, and his wants flexed along with the hardening muscle of stallionhood.

Now and again he would pause in his travels to sniff the fallen skeleton of a stallion who had challenged the red leader. Ants, maggots, and crows had picked the bones clean. The skull lay grinning in death.

Maturing, his neck arched in beauty; his eyes now carried fire and they burned like coals when he smelled the red stallion's mares. Raising a front hoof, he pounded the earth in warning, because power had gathered within him; his strength was ripe, cocked, and ready.

At three years, the young white stallion attacked at full charge and took all the mares for his pleasure.

After killing his sire.

BOOK

ONE

# CHAPTER
## 1

FLORIDA 1932

"GRAB TIGHT," THE CHUTE MAN WARNED.

I nodded, unable to answer. Whenever I'm scared, this half-eaten taste rises from my belly and fills my throat, like I was fixing to drown in sour milk.

*Eight seconds,* I reminded myself. *You only have to stick for eight.*
Using a left-hand grip, I tightened the leather thong that was now completing three loops across the cup of my left glove. Knuckles back, close to my crotch, palm forward. Beneath me, I felt the burning body heat of the angry animal I was about to ride.

As he snorted, it sounded more like a roar.

He was a big black curly-headed Galloway, and right now, we were smelling each other. His smell was hot and mean. A rodeo smell.

I didn't know what mine was.

One thing certain, I was grateful that my older brother Tate wasn't anywhere near the chute, telling me that I was twisting my wrap wrong. Tate Bodeen was probable in his seat, in shade, up yonder in the rodeo grandstand and watching my every mistake. He rode bulls and broncs like they were no more than the little painted critters on a merry-go-round.

Swallowing the cud that climbed into my throat, I forced it down again.

*Eight seconds.*

A million miles distant, the announcer was telling the crowd who I was and the name of the Galloway bull I was now sitting on.

"Folks," blared the loudspeaker, "keep your eyes on chute number two. It's fifteen-year-old Ladd Bodeen, about to make his first appearance on . . . Crankshaft!"

From the corner of my eye, I could see the two rodeo hands cinching the bite strap, to hurt and enrage the bull. Behind him, just as the gate swings open, a third man would give the bull's testicles an electric shock with a prodder. I fought the urge to climb off, now, while there was still time to sneak somewhere and hide. Please, I was begging God, don't let me cry. Ever since I could remember, Tate had threatened to cuff my face whenever he'd caught me in tears.

"No whimpering," he usual said. "Be a Bodeen."

With my free hand, my right, I yanked the brim of my Stetson down tighter, closing my eyes to pretend that it wasn't about to happen. My teeth clamped, trying to do everything the way Tate said, in order to measure up.

To prove out a man.

In my crotch, I felt the hot watery rush of fear suddenly pouring into my underwear and my jeans. I glanced down. The light washed-out blue denim clouded darker. One of the men noticed it. His gloved hand smacked my shoulder.

"I done it too, boy. More'n once."

Tate wouldn't have been so understanding. In a way, my brother would have rubbed my nose in it, like pushing a puppy's face into a wet carpet. Tate and I were ten years apart. Ten years, and several planets, even though we both lived at home on our Florida cattle ranch, the Buckle Tee.

"You ready, kid?"

Lean forward, I told myself. Keep your right arm high in the air and don't make a sissy's grab for a second hold.

I nodded. "Turn him loose."

The gate opened.

As the electricity jolted him, I felt it shock me too. The huge hunk of animal heat felt like flame, and was swollen with hatred and agony.

He charged.

The gate, even though operated quickly, had not fully spread, and the high latch board tore at my right leg, almost wiping me off. The five-piece rodeo band started to play, as usual, but I only heard their first brassy note. Leaving the ground, the bull made his first leap, taking off north but landing facing south, swapping ends. My eyes were suddenly squinting upward into a bright Florida sun. As his hoofs thudded into the sand, I felt the arched cleaver of his backbone slicing me into halves. My rectum burned like fire.

"Stop, please stop," I was trying to say aloud. "Oh God . . . God . . . please, please, please."

There is no braking a rodeo bull. There are no reins, no ignition key, no saddle, no lanyard hooked to his nose ring. He is wild and free, frightened by the crowd, the confinement, the blaring blast of band music, plus the pain . . . and the cause of it all: the enemy, a rider on his back.

Crankshaft, after three jumps, began to spin, and with us spun the entire world. Caught in a blur of whirling dirt, frozen in fear, my entire body was hurting to the point of madness. His pain and mine interlocked, opposed, torment embedded in torment. Twice a second, my neck and backbone snapped like a whip. I was a snake caught between the jaws of a head-shaking dog.

None of Tate's advice could I remember or apply. Realizing dimly that my brother was watching made it all worse.

The bull's spin was too fast, too tight for me to counter. Instead of leaning to the inside, I felt my upper body being pulled to the outside, my inside leg losing its hold. Something hateful was kicking me in the privates, harder than I could endure. Every part of me left him, except my grip hand, which was still tightly thonged within the leather loops. My bootheels dragged through the dirt, moving me backward, my left elbow and forearm above me, fingers warped by the brutality of their impossible position on the bull's hump. There was a horse near me, and a rider. Two horses. They were trying to pin a furious 2800-pound animal between them, to loosen the bite strap, and to correct my body enough to free my hand.

A hoof stepped on my ankle. Once, then again.

My hand free, I fell.

Tumbling beneath the bull's body, I tried to scream, but my mouth was filled with arena grit and the foul-tasting dust from dried manure. Vomit filled my throat, then reversed itself as my mouth closed. Hot fluid streamed out of both my nostrils. Sand was smarting my eyes, but I partly saw Ringo, the Kickaloo Rodeo clown, forsaking his barrel of safety and come running to attract Crankshaft's attention.

"Good try, kiddo," somebody said. It was one of the hazers, the older cowboys on horseback.

Lying flat, my face in the dirt, I waited for the sweeper crew to handle its job; that being, to haze the bull away from a fallen rider and into the exit chute with its double gate opened wide.

I didn't dare to move, or even to raise my head enough to look around. Figuring that my back and hand got busted, and maybe my ankle too, best I keep myself flat prone. Panting, I lay there hidden in pain and feeling the dirt sticking to my sweaty face; and worse, knowing that my brother was staring at me. Eyes closed, I could read his sober expression. He even spat. Then, in my mind, Tate was shaking his head as if to admit that his kid brother, the one he so often called a female name, could never begin to meet manhood.

"Lady . . ." I almost heard him saying, as I continued to heave, face down, into the arena sawdust and earth, wiping my mouth and face with handfuls of soil so that, when it came time to stand up, my vomit wouldn't show.

My fingers clawed the ground.

How, I was wondering, could I dig a hole and weasel into it? But there would be no escape from Tate Bodeen. Never had been. Since the age of two, I'd had no mother to run to. The accident took care of that. With my nose in the dirt, I tried very hard to remember her smile we hadn't seen for thirteen years. My mother's face had been pretty, I recalled. Like music, her voice had sung to me, even when she was only talking, or reading me gentle stories out of a picture book. And poems.

I felt hands.

These were not my mother's hands. Yet they were not unkind. Only firm. Insistent.

"Okay, kid . . . you're mostly frighted to death. Can't say I blame you. For fifteen, you're still a skinny ways off from a growed-up man. But you done a decent try. A good lick at it."

The band had stopped, and the rodeo crowd was clapping joylessly, the kind of dutiful applause people award to a loser. No cigar. I'd never expected to capture any prize money, but if I could only win a belt buckle, one that had the Kickaloo Rodeo insignia, it might be enough to satisfy Tate.

No, it wouldn't. Nothing I could do would ever please him. Tate didn't realize how much I wanted to make him proud of me.

On my feet, I searched for my hat, found it, dusted it off and limped slowly toward the fence. It seemed like a long walk, near to a hike. It's always that way, Tate had said, when a rider gets spilled, and it seems a mile longer than eight seconds. My ankle hurt worse than a fury and my left hand didn't hurt at all. It only prickled. Beyond that, nothing. But I wasn't going to mention any of the misery to Tate.

The fence was still twenty feet away.

Around me, the crowd had turned mute, yet I felt hundreds of eyes staring, silently laughing. Except for one person, Tate Bodeen, I was sure as my hand reached for the whitewashed board of the fence, was not laughing at all. He'd be sitting soldier-straight, eyes forward, his chin pointed defiantly at the center of the arena as though it were a target, one to be fought, and dominated.

As I slowly crawled up the fence, over, and then down the outside, a friendly face came forward to greet me. His name was Gusher Plant, an old man who worked on our ranch and had for a long number of years, and he was about the closest thing I had to a grandfather.

"A noble try, Laddy," he said.

He rested a twisted arthritic hand on my shoulder, very lightly, as though he knew I was smarting all over, and that included inside as well as out. Pulling a faded bandana from a hip pocket, the old cowboy started to wipe the grit off my face. What I really wanted wasn't Gusher's attention. Instead I was hoping that my brother would come looking for me, to tell me that I'd at least stuck my level best on that bull.

But he didn't. I ached for some brotherly friendship so much that the hurt of it in my mind was more painful than the hurting in my body.

I wanted Tate.

# CHAPTER 2

GUSHER NUDGED ME.

An hour had passed, and the two of us were now railbirds, perched side by side on the high arena fence to take in the action. But I didn't care much because it hurt so bad to breathe. All over.

"Ladd," he said, "you got two more tries. Your entry fee allows you three bulls."

I winced.

Inside my mouth, I was still aware of the sick taste, and my body couldn't quite seem to quit trembling. At least the urine stain in my crotch had dried back to a lighter normal. But the thought of having to fork two more bulls was a mite more than courage could muster. My body wasn't built like my brother's. To me, Tate looked like the first six feet of a tall oak.

"Tate won't approve a quitter," the old man warned me. "But who cares."

As he spoke, he straightened his arm to a level, pointing a crooked finger at my brother over in the grandstand. Gusher's finger appeared to have got busted in three joints. Or in three saloons.

"I can't top any more bulls," I told Gusher. "I'm not thick

enough to be a bull rider, and I got sense enough to know it. There's other things to become in this world."

Inside, I would ante up half of my life to be like Tate Bodeen. Except for his hardness. I don't guess I wanted to turn myself into another crowbar.

"Well," Gusher snorted, "I s'pose you could always limp gimpy and do some moaning. Maybe that'll convince him that one bull for today was ample plenty."

"Yes," I said, "maybe so," knowing full well that my brother would expect me to ride my three tries, even if I was broke in three places, like Gusher. Well, tough luck, Tate. I wasn't going to break bones to please anybody.

"I'm glad you're off that bull," Gusher said. "Ever since that awful day, whenever I see a Bodeen on a horse, or worse, my hands sweat and I take a leak every ten minutes."

Before us, the Kickaloo Junior Rodeo was still in full swing, bulls and broncs, steer wrestling, and calf roping. One particular loop settled high on a calf's head and broke his neck with a single yank. Some people in the crowd turned away and couldn't look as a man on a horse dragged the still-kicking calf out of the show area.

Gusher patted my knee once. "Don't fret about old Tate," he said dryly. "He's got a disposition mean enough to peel paint. But he ain't man enough to spook you." The old man paused to clear his throat. "I had me a try or two at a rodeo, years back. One bronc turned out to be more slippery than a wet seed, and he tossed me near to a mile. I had such a long walk back that I missed supper." He winked at me, knowing that I knew how hard he was trying to cheer me up. "That horse bucked like he'd been weaned on bedsprings. Near to stuffed my pants up into my hat."

The events kicked up lots of dust and it sifted up my nose. I sneezed. "Wow," I said, "it can't get any dustier than this, can it, Gush?"

Reaching over to me, he tugged my neck bandana up and around my nose and mouth, then did a likewise for himself. "Heck," he snorted through the faded red cloth, "you be only fifteen, Laddy, and you ain't never seen a real dusty spell."

I sighed. "I s'pose you have." According to Gusher Plant, he'd about drifted everywhere and tried it all. Tate claimed that Gusher sure had a proclivity for spreading cheer and manure.

Gusher nodded. "Sure enough have. About twenty years back, we had a dry spell right here in Florida that set records on aridity. It failed to rain for thirty-three days." Gusher yanked down his neckerchief.

"Dry?" I asked, waiting for old Gush to manufacture what he couldn't clear remember.

"Yup. But then, on the thirty-fourth day, one single raindrop fell, hit me on top of the head and knocked me stone-cold." Before I could smile, he pointed a finger at me. "You'll never guess what the other cowhands had to do to revive me back to reason." He uncorked a slow grin. "They throwed a bucket of sand in my face."

I couldn't help laughing.

"Honest?"

"Cross my heart, Laddy. Turned windy too, enough to flap a wet shirt. Got so stiff that all the chickens kept their rumps to the breeze. I saw a hen lay the same egg twice."

At that one, I near to toppled myself off the fence rail. And about stopped hurting.

"Almost blowed away every dang chicken we owned on the Buckle Tee. In fact," Gusher went on, "I saved those hens by feeding 'em lead buckshot to weight 'em down to earth."

My giggle spurred Gusher's chatter, all of which avoided the truth. Yet it didn't much matter. It was Gusher's way. I'd known him ever since I could recall. Tate claimed that Gush usual talked to delay or dodge work, but then Tate Bodeen could outwork two men and a mule. Gusher said once that Tate had a chore for a life and an oath for a benediction.

Gusher went on talking, pointing, saying something or other about the next event, commenting that there wasn't enough glue on a kid's britches, but I wasn't listening to Gush any longer.

I was watching Sue Louise Hartberry.

We went to school together; that is, on the days that I managed to attend. Sue Louise was fourteen, a year younger than I was, and she told everybody that she was already a woman. To hear her gave me an itch for manhood.

The feeling was a mite like hives.

Right now, in order to appreciate her, I had to turn my head and glance over my shoulder. She was standing not more than fifty feet away, displaying a blouse that might have been bought a size too small. Her clothes were so tight they must have caused cussing to squeeze into. She sure was a whistler.

From up in the grandstand, in the shade where the seats cost near a day's wages, the announcer raised his electric bullhorn. "Jimmy Dee Dolan, out of gate number one, on a new bull . . . Undertaker's Pal."

I paid little mind to the rodeo. Sue Louise was talking up Bill Tarky, a boy of about seventeen or eighteen who'd recent rode over on his motorcycle. He gunned the throttle at her, like his cycle was calling to its mate, and it didn't make me admire him a whole lot. Going real easy, Tarky rode his machine around and around Sue Louise, in circles, kicking up gravel with its rear tire. I felt my fist doubling, hardening, yet I knew better than to stand up against Bill Tarky. I'd have come up a second best.

When he stopped circling, he inched forward on the black seat, to make room, and she swung her leg behind him, sitting close, her arms around his chest and her breasts pressing against his back. It made my teeth grit. Maybe if I owned a motorcycle, one that was bigger and dusty as Bill's, she might allow to ride behind *me*. I'd hustle her right along Main Street and smack through the center of Kickaloo, to show every eye in town that Sue Louise Hartberry was *my* girl.

Not that she was, exactly. To my recollecting, I'd spoken to Sue Louise one time. She'd mentioned the weather on the school bus and I'd worked up the gumption as to allow it was humid.

"Right sticky weather," she'd said.

"Hot," I'd agreed, a regular poetic Robert Burns at conversation. And that single word had been, thus far, the extent of our courtship.

Sue Louise and Bill roared off on his stupid Harley, the pair of them on one seat, fitting closer than a couple of stacked spoons.

Gusher poked me.

"Turn around," he sort of grunted, "and forgit all your whang-doodle ideas about that filly in heat. It'll melt off. Love is a lot like bean gas. Time's got a way of tooting out the pressure."

"You ever been in love?"

"Indeed so." He gave my shoulder a friendly punch. "Aplenty of back-and-forths I took on that old porch swing. Fact is, I was sort of smitten about ten years ago, by a widow woman. Her name was Gertrude McGill."

"Pretty?"

Gusher Plant shook his head. "Naw. Just the opposite. So blame ugly that her looks could only be described by throwing up." He paused to suck at his teeth. "But it was her cooking that spunked *me* into a notion."

"Was Gertrude a good cook?"

"Terrible. Her coffee you had to stir with a hammer. It was thicker than hot mud and smelled worse than a sundown boot. To top it off, Gertrude usual wore a sorrowful expression, somewhere between the front of a courthouse or the hind of a jail. But her cookery . . . whenever she'd prepare a stew, it was so near to poison the Seminole Indians used to dip their arrows in it."

Laughing, I shook my head, not believing a word yet hankering to hear Gusher tell it. "And this was the Gertrude you took sweet on?"

"That's right, Ladd."

"How come?"

"Well, because with a woman like Gertrude, a man can't git to become too matrimonial serious."

It was all I could do to perch on the top rail. Gusher Plant sure could knot a few kinks into the cord of truth.

"Where's this Gertrude lady now?"

Gusher rubbed the gray stubble of beard on his jaw. "Well, I don't guess she's no place except still in jail. A real pity . . . packing a woman off to prison over such a flimsy matter." He sighed. "All she done was shoot a lawyer."

Gusher could make anybody laugh, except for Tate and Mrs. Skagg, our cook and housekeeper.

"Hey," the old man said, "if I can see straight, that's your pal about to emerge out of gate three."

I looked. Gusher was right. Buddy Collitt was up, and ready.

"Folks," roared the bullhorn, "coming out of gate number three, young Buddy Collitt . . . on a bronc you people all seen perform here aplenty of times . . . Spine Cracker."

The gate opened. Buddy gave a good ride, holding the white rope tight, free arm high and fanning air, boots forward, the rowel wheels of his spurs raking the horse's shoulders, his lean body swaying and giving each time Spine Cracker met ground. "Stick him, Buddy!" I hollered.

The band was really turning it on, perhaps inspired by the ride Buddy Collitt was giving us all to witness. The buzzer sawed the air above the music and the crowd hooted its appreciation. About five minutes later, I saw my brother congratulating Buddy, who wasn't even a year older than I was, on his successful ride.

Tate, who liked winners, even threw a friendly arm around Buddy's shoulder.

# CHAPTER
# 3

"LET'S CLIMB DOWN," GUSHER SAID.

We did. It felt restful. No matter how many positions a fanny tries on a fence rail, it eventual starts to feel like a numb waffle.

I watched Gusher Plant tug a small sack of Bull Durham from the pocket of his faded-blue work shirt, and then select a thin cigarette paper which he rolled part of the way under and around his first finger. He poured tobacco, licked the paper's edge, and rolled a smoke almost in one easy motion. His teeth and free hand yanked the drawstring closed.

"There," he said, inspecting the bag's snug-tight little mouth. "Dryer than a nun's kiss."

Gusher's cigarette was far from straight, being as crooked as the finger that had molded it. A cigarette with knuckles. With one flick, Gusher's thumbnail ignited the blue wooden match, causing it to hiss sulfur and spurt flame. One deep drag of smoke and the old man had his cigarette working. But after only a pull or two, Gusher tossed it to the Florida sand, grinding it out with an unshined boot.

He spat. "Dang smoke," he said, "tastes mean enough to pleasure a Texan."

Hunkering down, leaning my spine against a fence post, I looked up at Gusher. "Is it honest true," I asked the old man, "that you used to be from Texas, and then rode a wagon from there clean to Florida?"

"Sure is true. But not on a wagon. I arrived at the Buckle Tee riding a polar bear and using a rattlesnake for a whip. Then I picked a fight with a gator and even offered him first bite. After that, I sat myself down on the red-hot coals of a campfire, ate a cactus, and drank half a gallon of turpentine. Your folks asked me where I hailed from, so I natural confessed with pride that it was Texas. But, I told 'em, people are turning so mean out there that a few of us softies had to clear out."

An old rodeo cowboy limped by, one of the hazers, toting a ragged saddle blanket on his shoulder. Gusher eyed him with not much jealousy.

"Laddy," he final said, "you don't have to search through that poor waddy's pockets to know his condition. I'd wager he's as busted as most of his bones." He sighed. "I'm sort of thankful that you and your brother compete only once a year. Hitching to a rodeo circuit is chasing poverty on a lame leg. No sure profit in owning a racehorse neither. A man don't break a horse near as often as a horse can break a man. You'll wind up broke as the Ten Commandments."

While I was still seated and leaning against the fence post, I worked off my right boot. It wasn't surprising to see my sock wet with blood. Peeling it down to halfway, I inspected how my hide had been scraped to raw by the bull's hoof. But right now, there was little doctoring I could do, except to yank my sock up again and ease on my boot.

Gusher winced. "Well, I don't guess you'll kick up much of a two-step at the dance tonight. Not on *that* ankle."

"Don't tell my brother," I said. "There's no call for Tate to know about it. Hear?"

He nodded.

"Besides," I said, "I'm not going. First off, I can't dance better than a stumble, and second, my body hurts like I'm already dead and burning."

Behind us, out in the arena, a couple of old cowboys on horseback were dragging the dirt to smooth it, pulling a plank with their ropes. Little else was happening.

"Yes indeedy," Gusher said. "All you gotta do is keep clear of horses and bulls to think straight and walk level."

For some reason, I suspected that Gusher Plant was remembering my mother, a lady he knew for more years than I did. It happened when I was coming on two. Or beyond. Just a toddler. So I never got to know her at all. And there sure wasn't any knowing of Papa. Not since the tragedy. I'd grown up in the same house, on the Buckle Tee, but all I saw of Sam Bodeen was a silent man who sat in a chair with a light blanket over his knees, sometimes holding my mother's hairbrush.

Every day I'd visit Papa, trying to reach him. This I had tried for years and years. With no result. "Come back, Papa." Those were the three words I said to him more than anything else. Yet my father, Sam Bodeen, didn't want to come back to us, or couldn't.

Tate, Gusher, and Mrs. Skagg, who handled our kitchen, told me most of the story of how I sort of lost both my parents on that one awful day, thirteen years ago. Mama died. Papa lived, but hardly spoke another word to anyone, except me.

"Howdy again, folks," the grandstand bullhorn announced. "Please do return to your seats so's we can continue our final event of this afternoon . . . bronc riding!"

Gusher and I reclaimed our cheap general-admission seats on

the fence rail and watched. Mr. Jim Bob Grading, the man who owned the Kickaloo Rodeo and put on the entertainment, sure could think up some crowd-pleaser names for his bucking stock. Names like Neck Wrecker, War Dance, Poncho Villain, Dirty Hairy, and Rib Snapper.

During the show, however, my mind kept wanting to know what had happened thirteen years ago, to my parents, back when I was only two.

"He's a tough one," Gusher said, squinting through the July dust at a youngster who'd eaten quick dirt off the back of a bucker. "Not in the money, but a dang solid ride."

Somehow, I wasn't fully watching. My mind was home.

Out behind our house there was a slight rise in the land, a knoll, and on it grew one giant of a live-oak tree. Beneath it was a grave, and a headstone made of wood with a name Tate had carved into it.

Lola May Bodeen
1888–1919

At the age of thirty-one years, my mother died, and lay buried there. Never a day passed that Tate Bodeen, despite how tired and burnt from the Florida sun, didn't stroll up that knoll to our mother's resting place. He'd kneel, remove his sweat-stained hat, bow his head and keep silent. My brother never said much about praying. He seemed to handle it without words. Before rising, Tate usual patted the earth with his hand, only a few times, as if to keep Mama warm and safe.

Tate was lucky. He had known our parents some years. My brother knew our pa, Sam Bodeen, when he could talk and managed the ranch. All I'd had, really, was a mound of weather-hard sand on a hill; and a man with a blanket, holding a woman's hairbrush, staring off into clouds of memory. There didn't appear to be much left of Papa to know. His face was as vacant as an empty store.

One time, alone in our barn, I'd found a dried shell of a snake. Dead skin. The snake had shed itself and crawled away. Sam Bodeen had crawled away too. And gotten lost.

So I wanted to find him and bring him home. He wasn't under the blanket. My father was somewhere else, thirteen years ago, watching my mother's death and then wanting to die alongside her. I figured what had happened wasn't anyone's fault. Papa, I guess, had thought different. He blamed himself.

Although my brother visited Mama's grave each day, he never went near Papa. Or even mentioned his name. It was a grudge Tate was holding in the hardness of his heart. A morning never arrived that I didn't visit with my father, but I talked to a man who rarely responded, except to turn me an empty face. Sometimes he would smile at me, as though he understood things I shared with him.

"Tate's busy, Papa," I'd lie to him. "Soon as he gets time, he'll stop around to talk to you. Honest he will. Right now, he's got the Buckle Tee to ramrod, so please be patient. Hear?"

I wondered if Sam Bodeen heard. Still, even if he couldn't, I promised myself that I'd never quit trying.

My mind, or half of it, was listening to a rodeo crowd's cheer. I sort of woke up to pay attention to whatever it was Gusher Plant had been chattering about. He usual talked all the time, awake or asleep, and Slim, the other hand on the Buckle Tee, mentioned that not much of Gusher's air was saved for respiration.

Off to my right, I spotted Tate and waved my arm to him. He sort of nodded. Then I saw Tate walking our way, with purpose, like he had words for us. Mostly, I was guessing, for me.

Even before he got close enough to us to allow conversation, there was no doubt in my mind what subject Tate would tackle. Dreading it, my stomach clenched up real tight. With his hands hooked into his studded belt, my stocky brother stared up at me, as I was still on the fence with Gusher Plant.

"You whole?" Tate asked me. "Or in sections?"

I grinned, pleased that he cared enough to inquire. "About put back together. Crankshaft was a ton too much animal. But I didn't bust anything except my self-respect."

Tate spat tobacco juice into the dust. "I bought you three tries." As he spoke, the thickness of his neck seemed to redden. "Unless the bull painted you yellow. Three tries."

I nodded. "I know. Thanks."

"So," he said evenly, "I don't guess you're fixing to mount the other two." He sighed. "Maybe it's best. You ain't a whale of a lot of help as is, and with a broken butt you'll be uselesser."

"Leave the boy be, Tate," Gusher horned in. "He done his righteous best out there today. I seen it and so did you."

Tate's eyes narrowed. "Gusher," he said quietly, "I don't exactly recollect begging you for an opinion. What's between Laddy and me is a family matter, and what you cogitate about it doesn't amount to squat."

Next to me, I felt Gusher's body flinch, then stiffen, as if he'd been struck full in the face by a rock pie.

"No offense," the old man muttered, as though giving my brother, his boss, a halfhearted apology.

"Nope," said Tate. "Leastwise not yet."

I understood why Tate was firm with people. Because he was younger than I was when it happened. The accident. Younger, but a good deal tougher, soon enough. Even so, he had been a kid of twelve who suddenly had to take over a ranch, years ago, and I never knew anyone else who could have done it, and held us all together.

Tate had. So he was used to giving orders, expecting his commands on the Buckle Tee to be obeyed without question by Gusher and Slim and Mrs. Skagg. Especially by me. For thirteen years, I followed Tate Bodeen around, trying to keep up, and also willing to learn why such-and-such a command was given. Not to mention looking up to my brother like he was the only god I knew.

As soon as my mother had been buried, Tate's hand took a hold on matters, gave the orders, paid bills, made all the deciding. Some of his decisions had been wise, others less so. Yet nobody ever doubted which direction my brother marched. He never once considered going sideways.

Tate was a due-north soldier.

As I sat on the rodeo fence, looking down into his rawhide face, he took an easy step forward. Only one. "If you're considering trying two more bulls, forget it," he said. "We all seen enough Bodeens die or cripple."

"Thanks, Tate."

He shrugged, placing a boot on the bottom rail, then leaning into a bending knee upon which he momentarily rested an elbow.

"That old bull," he said, "near to tore you away from assembly."

I nodded. "He certain did."

Tate shook his head. "When I saw your hand was caught in its hold, there wasn't a thing I could do . . . except to call myself a fool for convincing you to enter." I felt better. But then he squinted. "You and me, we're of the same parents, but that's about it."

In a way, it was an insult, my brother's way of telling me that I wasn't ready to be a man yet, and might never be. People who knew our family called my brother another Sam Bodeen. Before the accident, Papa had been an iron man. Harder than other men. But these were things I would never learn firsthand, not by sitting quietly beside my father, a gray-haired man with a blanket over his knees, saying little or naught.

Inside the arena, a bronc went down hard, and I heard its spine snap. In a minute, a rifle shot, then another, told us that the bucking horse had to be destroyed. A yoke of oxen were brought in to drag the dead animal away. Then a kid, the rider, exited from the dusty arena, his face ashen-white, mouth open. Dropping the saddle he was carrying, he sat down, and held his body to keep from shaking. My brother saw it all.

"Not everybody can take it," Tate said. "Some'll best fold up and wilt like a capon."

He walked away.

# CHAPTER
# 4

"UP."

Even in my sleep, I not only heard my brother's commanding voice, but responded to it. Eyes open, I rolled out of bed, figuring by the lack of July daylight it wasn't quite five o'clock.

Tate was dressed. Boots on, he was ready to kick Monday morning and spit in its eye. And I'd gone to bed before he'd come home last evening.

"I suppose you took in the dance in town," I said, pulling on a sock. "How'd that new band sound?"

"Less like music. More like a train wreck."

Without wasting more words, my brother left. Tate Bodeen wasn't a man to fritter air on conversation. I stood up. From about head to toe, my body was hurting, like I'd been run over by a slow wagon. Every step was more groan than progress.

Downstairs in our kitchen, as angled as a person in a needle-point sampler, Mrs. Skagg stood at the big Acme American cookstove, one that she would often refer to as the Black Devil. I smelled bacon, eggs, coffee, toast, and steamy white grits, plus the clean-home aroma of Mrs. Skagg herself.

"Morning," I said.

Handing me my breakfast, her reply was, "Plate's hot." She passed it my way without bothering to look at me. The two eggs were shinier than pebbles in a stream.

I toted my plate to the table and sat beside Gusher. Across from me, Slim Service and Tate were whacking into breakfast like it had to be destroyed. Pouring some of Mrs. Skagg's coffee into a white mug, I tasted a first cautious sip. Strong enough to strip varnish. Forcing my first swallow, I looked across the kitchen, watching Mrs. Skagg kicking the stove.

"Smoke's worse'n Pittsburgh," she muttered.

Mrs. Skagg was small and lean. Inside, a kind and decent woman who cared about all of us, mended our clothes, and even quoted Scripture for our betterment. Although I really liked her, I'd never worked up the salt to tell her so. Somehow she attacked dirt, sloth, and sin with a mop and a skillet, or attempted to dunk all three into a sudsy tub, determined to keep a female order on this all-male cattle ranch.

Approaching the table and eyeing my meatless frame, Mrs. Skagg dumped more grits and another egg on my plate, then brought me a glass of buttermilk.

She spoke in a barren voice. "Ladd, as soon as you're outside your breakfast, take the mule into town. I'm near vacant on supplies."

"Okay."

"And," she added, "you're to parade yourself back here by dang noon, so's I can do supper."

"Yes'm."

From his empty plate, Gusher looked up at Mrs. Skagg. "No pie?"

"Last wedge of it disappeared in the night," she announced, looking at Tate without mentioning the culprit's name.

Mrs. Skagg liked all of us well enough, at least better than she liked the stove, but my brother was her obvious favorite. Had there been an extra slab of pie to clamp a lid on a breakfast, somehow she would have sneaked it to Tate's plate. Not because he was the boss. It was because he was "Mr. Tate" now, as she called him. I wasn't "Mr. Ladd" and never would be for at least another century. Far as I could figure, Mrs. Skagg believed in God, the Baptist Church, grits, President Herbert Hoover, and Tate Bodeen . . . but maybe not in that order.

As my breakfast fork was starting to work serious, I recalled times when I wanted Mrs. Skagg to put her arms around me, and hug me hard and warm. Yet it never happened and never would. She didn't hug anybody.

One exception.

A few years back, a stray old coonhound came to us here at the Buckle Tee, and Gusher Plant had named him Clubber because of a slightly deformed paw. Mrs. Skagg usual fed him table scraps, pretending how much she honestly disliked animals, and sometimes went so far as to shoo him off the kitchen stoop ahead of a broom. Clubber got kicked by a horse and right then crossed by a wagon wheel; the dog's intestines had been torn out, yet he was still alive and suffering worse than miserable. Tate came along, took a quick look at a hopeless situation, placed a boot on the dog's throat, lifted him up by the hind legs, and swung him against the trunk of a pine tree. Killed him instant.

The rest of us stood speechless.

"Mrs. Skagg," he'd said, "handle the sorrow," and walked quietly toward the barn. Returning, he tossed me a shovel. "Do it."

"Poor old Clubber," she kept saying over and over, after I'd helped her dig a grave for him. She'd picked out a spot for his burial, not too distant from her flower patch. Before covering the dead dog with dirt, she knelt and petted him some, stroking his torn ear. "I'll miss you, Clubber," she'd said, "because somebody ought."

After the two of us buried the dog, Mrs. Skagg opened up and told me one or two of her memories. Including the accident. My mother, according to Mrs. Skagg, had been sort of a frail woman, not thickset like my father. She tended to read books and to write poems and things, activities that people such as Papa and Tate wouldn't understand. Mama also had been much younger than Papa.

"She was a gentle soul, your ma," Mrs. Skagg had told me. "Delicate as Irish lace. She knew better than to tempt riding that red roan gelding, Strawberry, but your pa was calling her soft. Mr. Sam claimed he wouldn't own a horse he couldn't break enough for a woman to handle. So your mother hooked a leg over that ornery eye-roller. The last horse she would ever ride."

It had taken me years to learn about that sorry day. And there still remained holes, gaps, some facts yet to be uncovered.

"A good lady," Mrs. Skagg had allowed as we stood over the dog's fresh grave. "Your ma could thaw the winter out of your daddy, even out of *him* and all that hardness, and turn Sam green as spring grass." Mrs. Skagg had paused to shake her head slowly. "But I don't guess she could soften him to reason. Because he still shamed her aboard that toothy gelding on the final day of her life. She deserved more than that. On account your mother wed your pa on a wish and a promise, back when his shirt weren't hardly more than patches. He was a horse hunter, but she was near to a princess."

"Was she pretty?" I'd asked.

Mrs. Skagg had nodded. "Prettier than jam on a biscuit. A face like a Morgan filly. To me, your pa always favored a cooked rooster that was half-plucked. But not to her. Wherever she is,

Heaven maybe, Lola May Bodeen's forgiven him. Truly forgiven Mr. Sam."

"He loved her, didn't he?"

"Oh, indeed yes. But only in his fashion. More'n once I'd seen him touch the blush on her cheek with the tip of one work-dirty old finger, almost like he was afraid to caress a thing he doubted that he deserved."

After we had buried Clubber, the two of us strolled out beyond the barn to look at the sunset.

"Yes," Mrs. Skagg repeated after letting out a silent sigh, "Sam Bodeen loved that young woman. He'd look at her like a chuck-starved rider, eyes enshrining her with devotion, as though there be an empty in him that only she could fill."

Suddenly I was aware that I was sitting in our kitchen, at the table, staring down at an eggy plate. Tate, Gusher, and Slim had gotten up to tackle ranching and I'd never seen them go. At the sink, Mrs. Skagg was clattering the breakfast dishes.

Turning to look at me, she asked, "Well, how come *you're* so wordless?"

"Just thinking."

"On what?"

"Oh, nothing much," I lied.

"I don't believe it." She banged the black iron skillet with a scrub brush. "Kids are always full of wondering. People my age become too boiled out to dream, awake or abed. Not you. Ladd, you favor your mother in more ways than looks and build. Tate is merely Sam Bodeen all over again, but not you, thank goodness."

Suds sputtered up and out of the sink onto the unpainted boards of our kitchen floor. Looking down, I could see how shiny the nails were. Around one particular nail lay a gray strand that had pulled from Mrs. Skagg's busy mop, as though this one little raveling had gotten separated from all the others, to spend its life alone. I smiled. Either that or it decided to split from the herd and have its own faraway adventure.

It made me wonder if I'd ever have the bowels to hightail off the Buckle Tee and see the world. Or see Florida.

Facing me, her back to the sink's curved and pouting lip, Mrs. Skagg was wiping red shiny hands on a muslin towel. "You never told me complete about the Kickaloo Junior Rodeo yesterday. How'd you do?"

"A bull chawed me up and spat me out."

"S'pose your brother watched it all."

I nodded. "He was there. It's about the first day off he's taken since last fall."

Mrs. Skagg kept wiping her hands, even though they were dry. "Tate deserves a smattering of Sunday sporting, and maybe even a Saturday night in town to yahoo mischief. He's still young, you know, even if he handles a man's job and a man's worry. Tate'll keep a home around old Gusher, Slim, you and me. He's tougher than fence wire. Oh golly, how I pray he'll meet up with a gal who'll wink at him, and make him feel like he's a cat rolling in sunshine."

My face felt its own smile, because Mrs. Skagg would never guess how poetic she could be. She herded feelings into the drab shadows of her life.

"Well," she grunted, "don't sit there flashing a boy's grin at *me*. Best get yourself cracking in the direction of Kickaloo, on account I got us a list of needs longer than Gusher's yarns. And if Dolbeck nags you for cash money, you trigger both barrels at him, and pronto. Tell him that the Buckle Tee don't owe a penny to nobody. We ain't the fanciest outfit in Florida, but we don't cheat people into forever, and never will. And you may remind Mr. Dolbeck that I'm just as good a Baptist as he is. Hear?"

"Yes'm, I hear."

"Stop in at the grocery. Old man Schultz has got fresh pickles that'll capsize the Ark. Don't get 'em by the jar. They're too dear priced thataway. Make him fish each one up and out of the barrel and pay bulk. Most important, don't buy one cussed item that ain't on my list. You perform exact as I order and I'll bake you a surprise. One with raisins."

"I will."

"All right then. Fetch yourself upstairs and brush your teeth with that toothbrush I give you last Christmas. I know it's July, and that contraption ain't been exercised more'n a dozen times. But do it. Then it's outside for you, harness Evelyn, point yourself toward town and take a purchase on Monday."

For some reason, Mrs. Skagg smiled at me, her grin spreading open to exhibit one canine fang, upper left, which had been nudged out of line by its chunky brethren.

"And take care," she said. "By the time you find yourself home, around noon, I'll have your daddy up and dressed, so you can talk to him."

I nodded. Without brushing a single tooth, I headed out to the barn to drape a harness over Evelyn, our mule. But before leaving the Buckle Tee, I stole ten seconds to see Papa, just to kiss his sleeping face. In alarm, his eyes opened wide.

Yet when they softened, I figured I was welcome.

# CHAPTER
# 5

"GIT UP, EVELYN."

As I gently snapped the reins to her flank once more, the mule and I were entering Kickaloo, and Evelyn figured we'd come far enough. Some folks claimed that Kickaloo wasn't much of a community, and never would be, yet it was the only town I'd ever seen, so I couldn't kick about Kickaloo.

From the wagon seat, behind Evelyn, I waved to a fellow I knew whose name was Canfield Horner, a boy with red hair.

"Hey there, Can."

"Hey, Laddy. How ya holding up?"

"Okay, I reckon. You playing any baseball this summer? If'n so, let me know, and I'll come watch ya hit a homer."

Canfield flashed me a thumbs-up sign. "You bet, Babe." Among baseballers, everyone was Babe these days, whether or not you were a big batsman like Mr. George Herman Ruth.

I'd been in Kickaloo less than two minutes when I heard a motorcycle, Bill Tarky's, and I couldn't resist turning around to see it. There he was, in a blue denim jacket, riding along Main Street free and easy, tooting his beep-beep horn at the girlies and pushing his goggles up on his golden curls, like he was Mr. Barney Oldfield, the famous speedcar racer.

"Howdy there, Anna June," I overheard him hollering, like he expected the whole dang state of Florida to kick up heels and throw undies in the air.

Then it happened. I saw Sue Louise Hartberry.

"Wow," I whispered to nobody in particular. She sure was a picture of pretty. It was like somebody actual took a plank and then whomped me across the belt, about six or seven times. Yet, despite the pain, there certain was a lick or two of pleasure.

What agonized me the most was when Sue Louise noticed Bill Tarky like he was the only doggone boy in the entire world. I saw her lower her eyes, then peek, to see if Tarky was actual looking in her direction. Sure was difficult to believe that Sue Louise was only fourteen. I don't guess she was older. But gosh, she certain couldn't have been a minute younger. Watching her, I tried to sit up taller than normal on the wagon seat, wishing our ranch mule was an Arabian.

Bill Tarky eased his motorcycle to a whoa and waved to Sue Louise.

"Let's go riding," he said.

Hearing it made my guts kink. It wasn't the easiest thing in the world to listen to.

As I pulled our mule to a stop and climbed down off the wagon bench, Bill or Sue Louise didn't seem to notice me. It was like I was morning mist that eyes could see through. So, with a shrug, I looped the reins a few turns around the upright handle of the wagon brake and entered the store.

The smell hit me. Dolbeck's Feed Store had a way of making your nose smile. Grain, malt, ice-cream salt, rye, oats, bolts of canvas, sunflower seeds, rolls of tar paper . . . it was all there in one aromatic blend. The plank floor was always gritty and caused a lot of Dolly's customers to feel like dancing. The side doors lay open, leading to the alley where a flock of fat brown sparrows were busy cleaning up the spilled oats and sorghum. Dolly's back was to me. He was busy with tack, straightening a hang of leather thongs, standing on a pair of pasture salt-lick blocks, one brown, the other white. The white block had tiny little stars in it where the sunlight made it shine.

"Howdy, Mr. Dolbeck."

Turning, he slightly nodded. "Morning." I wasn't a high-class customer worth wasting a smile.

"How's business?" I asked him.

"Not so doggone busy. It's the Depression. Money's gone somewheres, but there's not a merchant in town who can figure out exactly where. Sure ain't here in Kickaloo. Folks hereabouts can't conjoin a nickel and a dime."

"Tate says he can't honest complain," I lied, knowing how tough the times were. "We got a good healthy crop of calves this past spring on the Buckle Tee."

Mr. Dolbeck snorted. "For payment, I don't ring up calves. I take cash." There was a message in his voice. Either that, or a sermon. Our conversation was sort of a game of checkers. My first move bragged that our ranch was prospering, even if it barely hung on, and then Mr. Dolbeck countered with his move, about wanting to do cash business instead of credit in times of paltry. He knew our outfit was short on assets. Mighty short.

Hearing footsteps, I looked to my left to see another customer entering. It was Mr. Jim Bob Grading, the gentleman who owned several enterprises in town, including the Kickaloo Rodeo. As he approached, I was about to hand my list of purchases to Mr. Dolbeck, but I could see that an important customer would be waited on first.

"Well," said Dolly, wiping both hands on his gray apron, "what can I do for *you,* Mr. Grading?"

His order was extensive, lots of feed and grain for his rodeo stock, and I noticed that Mr. Dolbeck toted every single bag to Mr. Grading's wagon. In fact, he went so far as to order me to move mine, which I did, hearing Evelyn bray a complaint about the social injustice.

"Dolly," Mr. Grading asked, "you hear the latest hunk of news?"

"Probable not. Been too busy."

"Well, seems there's a band of horses roaming south of here. All running loose. Wilder than sin on Sunday."

"Who said?"

"Tobin Corbett told me. Said he counted near to maybe a dozen. He also claimed that he'd never before seen wild horses in Florida, but he did recent."

"Where they located?"

"At a place he calls Republic Flat. A wide-open range, good grass, and plenty of water. Tobin chased 'em in his truck, but on account he was a mite low on gas, gave up and quit. I sure would buy 'em, I told Tobin. Lost three horses yesterday, one calf, and a bulldog steer. And with August and September due to come along, I'd pay folding money for that band of roamers." Mr. Grading looked at me for the first time. "Say, aren't you Tate Bodeen's kid brother?"

"Yes, sir."

"Well now, sonny . . . listen up. You tell Tate that I pay immediate for horse stock, sight unseen, for rodeo or dog meat. Will you give him that message?"

I nodded.

"Tell him I'll buy 'em dead or alive. But if I got a choice, I'd cotton to see if any of those mustangs are possible rodeo broncs. Understand?"

"Yes, sir," I said again.

Mr. Jim Bob Grading pointed a finger at me. "Another thing. If he's making a drive toward town behind those mustangs, tell him to send you on ahead to open one of the arena gates, and then herd the entire band snug inside. Then close the gate and shoot the bolt. Tell your brother that soon's it's done he'll have money crackling in his hand inside of twenty-four hours."

I leaned back against a turpentine barrel. "I'll tell him. You want the whole band . . . mares, foals, every head, regardless of age or sound condition?"

"Every bag of bones he can haze in."

"Okay, Mr. Grading."

The man squinted one eye, resting an easy boot on a large coil of black rubber hose. "Might be a bonus, tell him. Maybe for Tate Bodeen there won't be an entry fee in September's Hoopla. A little something on the side." He winked a slow wink, as if asking me if I caught his meaning.

I did. "Yes, sir, Mr. Grading."

"Right now, Dolly, I best replace a few rodeo head. One of my toughest broncs, Buckshot, took ill this morning and wouldn't stand. Had to destroy him. No sense spending vet money on beagle chow."

I was curious. So I spoke up.

"Mr. Grading, my brother might want to learn how much money you're willing to shell out for *one* horse, so he can total his take in advance, or add up if it's worth the chase."

He spat into the dusty floor. "You got a head for business, son. What did you say your first name is?"

"I didn't say. You never asked me."

"Well, I'm asking. Tell me."

"I'm Ladd Bodeen." A thought crossed my mind, because there was something about Jim Bob Grading I didn't trust. So I hauled in a deep breath, held my nose, and jumped into business with both boots. "Before we go horse hunting, sir, I'll need some proof of a sale price on paper. Something in writing. Because we can't afford to go scamping all over Florida to bring in horses at a loss."

I held my breath. Yet I knew I'd made the wise move, because Mr. Grading had so foolishly announced that he needed the new stock. And the Buckle Tee sure needed the money. Were Mr. Grading to wait until late August or September, he'd be desperate and have to pay double, or even triple. In a sense, circumstances had backed him into a corner, against cactus.

Mr. Grading's eyes narrowed.

"Boy, you've got some tough on you. A coat of thick bark. You took your share of nerve, I'll give you that. Maybe you'll hatch into the kind of a horse hunter your pa was."

"Thank you, sir. But I still want to see an offer in writing, because nobody on the Buckle Tee can afford to round up a band of wild horses, bring 'em here, and then hear an offer of nothing or next to it."

"Say," said Mr. Dolbeck after one heck of a long silence, "you're only a boy. You best not be talking up to Mr. Grading thataway. It's not polite." He turned to Jim Bob. "Kids today, they don't know their place."

To my surprise, Mr. Grading walked to where I was standing and clapped a big hand on my shoulder.

"You're all right, sonny."

"My name's Ladd," I said. "And I would like *my* name on the agreement, instead of my brother's."

"Ladd . . . I got respect for a man, regardless of age or size, who can clutch business like a hawk. You'll do fine." Reaching into his pocket, he pulled out paper and one of those new fountain pens that carry their own ink inside, in some little secret tank. He wrote it all out. "There," he said, "you'll carry this guaranty that I'll pledge sixty dollars per horse, dead or alive. And if you can throw a rope on the stallion that leads that band, an extra hundred." He handed me the paper. "That's a quicker poke than you'll profit from your bunch of cows."

I slipped the paper into my pocket, offered my hand, and Mr. Grading took it, not guessing how close I was to wetting my trousers for the second time in two days.

Mr. Grading left.

So did I, after getting every item on Mrs. Skagg's list of supplies. As he filled my order, I took notice that Mr. Dolbeck treated me different, on a new level. "Anything else, Mr. Bodeen?" he asked, carrying a sack of oats to my wagon.

"That'll do," I told him. "Charge it. You know blessed well we're good for it, because no Bodeen's ever cheated you an owed penny. Right?"

Unwillingly he nodded. "Right."

Outside I saw Bill Tarky still talking to Sue Louise Hartberry, finally convincing her to climb behind him on his motorcycle. "Let's go, sweetheart," he said to her. Together, they roared away.

I tossed the reins to smack Evelyn, our mule, as we were about to point for home.

"Let's go, sweetheart," I said.

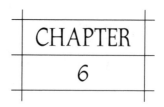

# CHAPTER
## 6

GUSHER WAS HONKING HIS HARMONICA.

The sound he was producing couldn't honest be called music. It was more like a burn or a cut.

Slim was singing. "Oh . . . the . . . moon shines tonight on pretty Red Wing. The moon is shining. My heart is pining."

The three of us were sitting a beat-up bench on the west side of the bunkhouse watching the sun back off from a tired day. Slim Service didn't know all the words to "Pretty Red Wing." He warbled the same verse over and over.

After about five futile tries on progressing beyond that, Slim quit singing and Gusher Plant mercifully stilled his harmonica, slapping it on his trouser leg to flush out the spit. Then he tried a turn or two of "Buffalo Gal," but not a whole bunch of it rang true.

Slim yawned. "Well," he said, "just maybe I'll go inside, wet my socks, and then turn myself into a Z. I'm so pooped out that if'n I blow on the lantern, I could jump into my bunk before the light goes out."

Slim departed.

That left Gusher and me, if you're counting.

"Gush," I said, "how far do you reckon it is from the Buckle Tee to a place called Republic Flat?"

Gusher Plant rubbed his white chin stubble. "Oh, I might estimate a hundred miles or so. Maybe a tad less. It's south of here, and distant. Florida is long country. How come you're asking? You're not fixing to wander down to Republic Flat, are ya?"

Hurriedly, I lied. "Gosh no."

"Nothing down so except real estate, all of it empty, wild, and good for gators but little else. I'd wager that Republic Flat be a place to stray away of," Gusher said, "unless you hanker to either live off cactus or git lost." Gusher was silent for a spell. "Funny," he said, "now that you mention it, I do recall a friend of your pa's. He lives down thataway, and maybe an inch beyond."

"What's his name?"

"Dodge Yardell."

"I've heard that man spoken of before. Maybe more'n once. It sort of rings a bell." I repeated the man's name softly. "Dodge Yardell."

"He sure is a loner. Ain't a animal or plant or a human that Dodge can't talent a likeness of, out of wood. Best doggone carver I ever did see, bar none. Even though I ain't seen him in a score of years, I do so clear remember much of his work. He could take a big old cypress tree stump and, with one knife, turn it into a wooden pony about the size for a child to mount."

"One knife?"

Gusher spat. "Yep. The blade and the handle were sort of set at an angle, kitty corner, not the usual way of where a blade continues the same line as a handle. Dodge Yardell called it a crooked knife. And, by golly, that's exactly how it looked. Pitiful crooked."

"You said Mr. Yardell's a friend of Papa's."

"A close friend. Short Callum too. Years back, they were rascals together, away before life turned so brown. I hear your father say his name, a number of times. Dodge Yardell. Then he'll smile. For your daddy, that be one hell of a rare occurrence, and it sure don't dawn every decade. Yet there it is, warming his face. A single remembrance of a friend."

"They were pals?"

"More'n that. They was *horse hunters.*" The old man stared at me. "Know what that means, Laddy? Together, they rode out into the Florida bush, years ago, to track and capture wild horses that maybe dated away back to the time when all those cussed Spaniards rode across these plains, killing and raping. And worse . . . pretending how doggone religious they were."

"How religious?" I asked Gusher.

"Not dang very."

"You're not religious at all, are ya, Gusher?"

"Nope. I like people better'n saints. Don't guess I believe in a hereafter. Instead, I believe in a here now. Learn to enjoy that, Laddy, and you'll lick life."

For some reason, my hand was rising to touch the pocket of my shirt, and I heard the rustle of the paper that Mr. Jim Bob Grading had handed me this morning at Dolbeck's Feed Store. I felt it. Still in my pocket, safe, all mine, a contract that just might work up handy. My face smiled. As old Mr. Grading allowed, I had some tough on me, yes indeed. A layer of thick bark. As I smirked, awash in my own cleverness, something that Gusher Plant was saying brought me back to a here now.

"Here comes Tate," he said.

Looking up, I saw my brother . . . thick, hard, and resolute, the kind of a young man generals raise from the ranks and forge into officers and leaders. Tate's voice was made to issue orders, to bark commands to men twice his age. In the case of Gusher Plant, three times.

"Howdy there, boys," Tate said. "Sure is a decent evening, sunset and all."

Knowing my brother, I figured he had not wandered down to the bunkhouse to discuss the majesty of sundown . . . oh no, not Mr. Tate. He would have a purpose, a goal, some premise that pointed as sharply as a compass needle. Standing at one end of the bench upon which Gusher Plant and I now were sitting, Tate rested a boot on the worn graying wood, took a deep breath, and let it out careful slow.

"Well," he said, "I don't guess I'd be too surprised if you waddies heard the news too."

He waited.

Seconds ticked by. "What news?" I asked him.

"This afternoon," Tate said softly, "I happened to be in Kickaloo, on business, and stopped in at Dolbeck's Feed Store." He looked down at me. "Baby brother," he said to me, "you certain enjoyed yourself one busy day."

"Well," I told him, "as Mrs. Skagg requested, I took the mule and wagon to town and stocked up on provisions, listened a spell to all the local gossip, and then Evelyn and I hauled back. We were home by noon."

Tate looked down at me, remaining silent. "Laddy," he said, "there's more to it."

I knew what he meant. No fibs. No storytelling. He wanted a pie-in-the-face honesty. So I gave it to him. Tate wasn't too often described as a kind or gentle person. Yet, not once in my lifetime, could I ever say he'd been dishonest. Tate Bodeen was as honest as a punch in the nose. Only more direct.

"Okay," I told him. "I was sort of jawing with Mr. Jim Bob Grading about some wild horses that are free grazing south of here, a place called Republic Flat."

"And?"

"He wants somebody to go round up the entire band and herd

'em toward Kickaloo, and he'll pay cash money for every one, dead or alive, with a bonus on the stallion."

"Well now," he said softly, "that's more like it. Congratulations. That was what I'd label as Bodeen straight."

Gusher Plant was looking first at my brother, then at me, as if wondering what in the name of tarnation the two of us were talking about.

Tate's following statement told him.

"Tomorrow morning," my brother said, "I'm fixing to ride south and hunt me a cash crop, a band of mustang horses."

I stood up, wishing I could be as tall and thick as Tate. "Good," I said, remembering how much bark I had on me, "because I just bet you'll round 'em all up." I sucked in a breath. "With my help."

Tate's voice was firm and even. "I'm going alone."

"If you do," I said, "you'll be riding a gamble. You're rolling dice. But if I'm along with you, we got us a guaranty, in writing, that we can market the stock dead or alive, with a contract price signed by the man himself, Mr. Jim Bob Grading."

Tate's mouth hardened into a thin line.

"I can't believe you," he said. "Ain't a horse buyer in all Florida who'd issue a purchase order on wild stock."

"There might be, Tate."

"Who?"

"Mr. Grading." Reaching up to my shirt pocket, I extracted the slip of paper, signed with a bold and inky J.B.G. "Here," I said. "It's mine. If you read it carefully, you'll see the name Ladd Bodeen. So if you're so all-fired fixing to ride off around sunup tomorrow, best you take me along. Because I got the guaranty. Right here. In your hand, big brother. Maybe I'm no bull rider, but I sure stuck on Jim Bob Grading for eight seconds."

Tate read the paper.

I could hardly hold a straight face as I noticed how Gusher Plant looked at me, then at Tate, then back at me again. "Think I'll sort of turn in," he said, as though this was another family puddle in which the old man didn't want to wet his boots.

Gusher left sudden.

That left the two Bodeens: Tate, the boss, who had been the ramrod of the Buckle Tee cattle ranch for thirteen years, facing his kid brother, me.

"Don't crowd me, Laddy," he said. "I'm dead-dog tired and my bones ache. To give you the straight of it, I'm too blame beat to take a bath in free beer."

I sensed what he was saying was true, because Tate worked harder than most men. He could ride circles around Slim and Gusher and then total up pennies. Add to that the number of after-sundown hours he spent at his desk, on records, numbers, and calves, and money we owed. Looking at him, I couldn't dislike Tate. He was as solid as Florida dirt. Tate Bodeen was the first man up and the last to close his eyes, day upon day. And if anyone ever said that there was no love in him, I'd stand up and claim the truth, how he loved the Buckle Tee, our land, and our mother who rested beneath it. He just never loved his kid brother.

These, of course, were matters I could not discuss with Tate. Sentiment wasn't to his liking. He was a dog killer, because nobody else could think of what to do, and muster the guts to do it. Tate could and did.

But right now, I had my own guts to exercise. And it was high time I stood up to Tate, so, hauling in another deep gulp of hot evening air, I spoke my piece.

"I'm going after those horses. And I intended to go with you, because this trip was *my* idea before it was yours." I paused. "It could be ours together."

"Not a chance."

"Why not?"

"Because you're more'n a mile away from manhood, and I can't figure you could cut it down there on the outback. It's rough country. I don't want nobody hurt. Our family has tasted its share of damage, more than plenty."

Hooking a thumb into my belt, I stared at him. "I'm going, Tate."

Tate's finger shot upward and then pointed into my face. "And I'm dead against it."

"That agreement signed by Mr. Grading is *mine,* not yours, and it proves that horse hunting for the Buckle Tee is sudden a two-man job." Pulling my thumb from my belt, I jabbed it at my chest. "You're looking at the other man."

"You'd do dang precious little except slow me down, Laddy. I'll have enough to worry on, without studying on how to keep you in one piece."

"They're not your horses. What you're forcing me to do is go alone, and maybe that's what'll happen, soon as you ride off this ranch. We can be partners. But no, you want it all your way, by orders of the high-and-mighty Tate Bodeen. You're not tougher than I am. All you are is bigger and ten years closer to dying."

His fist hardened.

For an instant, I thought that Tate was fixing to throw a punch at me. But then he slammed his right fist into the open palm of his left hand, as though he wanted to hurt somebody hard. Tate was used to getting his own way. Nobody stood up to him, not here, and not in Kickaloo. The truth was that I didn't hanker to head out on my lonesome.

"Like I said, it's a two-man job. You and me together. Sooner or later, you'll have to accept me as a partner, so it might as well be now. I'm going. And you best understand so. Come tomorrow, it's going to be Bodeen and Bodeen."

Tate bit his lower lip. "I never seen you so set."

I grinned. "Get used to it."

He almost smiled. "You won't tumble off your mount, lose the mule, or weep yourself to sleep when it turns dark?"

"Never. Not one time."

It was Tate's turn for a full sigh. "Agreed," he said at last. "I'm too done in to argue. But you got to keep up. None of your little sissy-boy bawling or whining. The first teardrop I see, and I'll strip you to raw naked, hawgtie you on your horse, and send you home. If this trek throws you, you'll not stumble away from it like it's only a few sorry seconds on a rodeo bull. You'll have to climb back on. Gusher and Mrs. Skagg won't be around to wipe the snot off your nose. Can you hack it?"

I nodded. "I'll hack it, Tate."

"We'll sudden see."

# CHAPTER
## 7

I WAS HEARING MRS. SKAGG.

Her voice sliced through my sleep, some foreign element, a noise that didn't belong in my fantasy dream of Sue Louise Hartberry and her cheerleader's legs.

All to the tune of Mrs. Skagg's telling me that I'd best be crawling out of bed, because Tate was already down at the corral, a saddle on his shoulder. And, unless I hopped up right now, and righteous sudden, there wouldn't be any breakfast. No coffee, no eggs, and no bacon. There would be only Tate's voice telling me that he had eaten his breakfast eggs and I wouldn't even hear as much as a hen's cackle.

"Up," she said, "and be about."

My clock read 4:35. The numbers on the dial tumbled around in their circle, a clock's sense of humor, as though laughing at me. Tate's face was the clock's face, and little clockish hands hung down from his nose like a Mandarin mustache.

"Come on. You'd best roll out."

In a daze, I searched for yesterday's socks, finding little more than confusion. Ah, one sock. Then another. They flew to my feet like homing pigeons. My clothes were screaming for sleep, and my belly for eggs and grits.

In less than a minute, I thumped downstairs to our kitchen, rubbing my eyes as I watched Mrs. Skagg dump a breakfast to an unheated plate. As I wolfed it down, looking at it with the half-open eyes of a sick chicken, my brother appeared at the kitchen doorway. A platter of food met his outstretched hand and then the pair of us butchered breakfast in silence.

"Let's go," Tate told me. "Little brother, you'd probable waste time watering a weed."

"Okay," I said, not bothering with a needed bowel movement, in order to sneak into my father's bedroom. His eyes were open, almost alert, as though waiting for my early-morning visit.

"Papa," I said, "you lie quiet. Tate and I are riding south to find some mustangs. Wild horses, Papa. We're going to bring home the entire band. Maybe even the stud. All of them." I wanted to tell him that we couldn't pass up a chance for some necessary money, but in case he'd understand, and worry, I didn't mention our sorry financial state.

In the gloom of his bedroom, my father blinked searchingly until he located my face. Mouth open, he was trying to speak, as if crying out to offer some piece of advice that my brother and I might use. A hard hunk of wisdom.

Gently, I touched his face.

"It's all right, Papa. We'll look after each other, because that's what brothers are supposed to do. Right?"

For a moment, in a trinket of time, I thought I saw my father's head nod, as though to say . . . *yes, watch out for each other, please do. Because you and Tate are my boys, my sons, seeds of my seed.*

"I have to leave, Papa."

Closing the door to his room, I joined Tate and Mrs. Skagg in the kitchen. My brother was busily stuffing a knapsack with corn dodgers, grits, strips of dried beef, dried plums, potatoes, carrots, and some salted ham. He added a packet of coffee and a sack of raw white beans.

"You fixed?" he asked me.

"Yes." Grabbing a hot biscuit, I stuffed it into my mouth, and then thought I'd jam extra biscuits into each of my two shirt pockets, so I did. The heat teased my chest.

We left by the kitchen door.

Seeing as it was still extra early, our bunkhouse was unlit. Inside, somebody snored. It had to be either Slim Service or Gusher Plant as they were its only occupants.

Tate tossed me a rope, then another. "Go catch us two horses while I diamond-strap some stuff on the mule. Not just any two . . . I want that bay mare for myself. For you, bring that buckskin gelding." I started to leave for the meadow on a run, but then Tate stopped me. "Whoa," he said. "You best not full-tilt charge at an animal unless you allow the job to spill our day to a waste. Go slow, Laddy. Approach easy. Take your time and you'll save us all time. Hear?"

"Yes, I hear."

Walking across the meadow, I was considering Tate's advice. It made more than a lick of sense. Even during the days in my life that I bitterly hated Tate, I'd had to admit, upon cooling, that what little he said was intelligent. Tate Bodeen was no fool. In a way, he was older than everyone else I knew, including Gusher.

Tate had been born old.

Overhead, there was still some moonlight, a shy moon, wondering if it could continue to compete with a soon-rising sun. Or should it back off graceful? Looking toward our barns, I could see my footprints across the light gray dew on the meadow grass. Inside my fingers, the horse ropes felt rough and bristling. I should have brought gloves. Tate had. My brother never forgot anything. Except me.

In about half a mile I spotted our band of horses, all six, all with a **BT** branded on a left hip. It stood for the Buckle Tee. Our cattle wore the same identification, plus an ear notch.

The horses saw me coming. Either that or they heard me, and smelled me. The six of them were standing, facing me, as though wondering why this particular Tuesday morning was commencing so early. Gusher usual claimed that animals could tell time, and that nobody knew the art of it better than a milk cow. Ranch horses must know too.

"Howdy," I said to the horses.

Wisely, I didn't walk directly at them, but headed sort of off to one side, in order to work my way closer without appearing to threaten them with a frontal attack.

"We don't need all of you," I said softly. "Only two, the buckskin and bay mare. So it'd be right neighborly if you'd step this way."

No, I didn't expect they would oblige, and they didn't. They just continued to stare, ears up and forward. I used up about two minutes to walk a complete circle around the entire string. Not a big circle. Horses tend to graze close to one another, even when two bands are divided by a fence. A horse wants to cozy other horses.

"Well now," I told them, "you know who I am, so don't spook and gallop away. My brother's waiting on us. You wouldn't keep a guy like Mr. Tate waiting. Me? Oh, I'm nobody at all. I'm not even Mr. Ladd, leastwise I wasn't to Mrs. Skagg this morning." I sighed. "When you're a skinny runt of fifteen who can't stick on a bull for eight seconds, nobody calls you anything . . . except for chicken chores and fetching."

I stopped. Maybe, I thought, it might serve best to stand quiet for a spell. The buckskin was curious, and he tossed his head a couple of shakes, as though trying to take a more accurate whiff of my smell. Sooner or later, one of the mounts would come to me. You can't find an animal more curious than a horse, according to Gusher, and that included cats and most ladies.

It happened quickly.

Gypsy, our oldest mare, began to walk toward me, very slowly, yet constantly moving closer and closer, taking her time. She was a chestnut with a slightly lighter mane and tail, and for ever since I could remember, she had dropped some beautiful foals. She'd breed true. Almost every colt or filly looked like Gypsy herself, and Tate sold them for a hefty price, especially when she'd drop a sorrel. As Gypsy came to me, I rubbed her nose and head, and then the bay mare decided to investigate too. If carrots or apples were being offered, no horse would want to miss out on easy treats.

"How does that feel? Good?" I asked the bay as I touched her face.

Both the mares felt damp with the dew of night, and would remain so until the sun dried them.

It was easy to slip a loop over the bay's eager head, and then, leading her along, I moved close enough to rope the buckskin gelding. He was less anxious to cooperate, not anxious at all. Head up, he fought the rope, burning my hands as it snaked through my fingers. Snaked was right. A rope actual does emit a hiss as it fangs at your raw skin.

"Come on, Buckskin," I said. "For a few days, you're going to be mine, let's pretend, so I'm calling you by a fitting name, Buckskin. And you best get used to working because we're loping a long way from the Buckle Tee."

It took some doing, but my determination won out, and I led both the bay and buckskin back to where my brother stood with an impatient expression on his face.

"I figured," Tate said in a mirthless voice, "you were taking the whole dang day off."

My brother wasn't open to hand out praise the way a Saturday-night sailor spends money. The fact is, had he greeted me with an approval, I'd have dropped both ropes.

"Saddle the buck," he said. His saddle slapped on the mare in a matter of seconds. Then he came to me, watched me struggle with the cinch, and shoved me aside, not politely. "This ain't a July vacation, boy, even if there's no school."

We headed south, riding between the two tall posts and under the weatherbeaten wooden sign with a **BT** on its arch. I handled Buckskin about as well as could be expected, while Tate rode ahead of me holding Evelyn's lead rope.

The mule snorted.

She planted both front hoofs, stopped, and nearly spilled Tate over backwards. And then I heard the noise, one I'd heard all my life in Florida, a buzzing, a warning that could chill a corpse. A rattlesnake struck at the mule's legs, making her white-eyed in fear. Rearing, she spun around as Tate turned the bay mare, and the mule's rear hoofs flew up high and hard. It sounded as if somebody blew a truck tire. A hoof caught Tate in the ribs. Falling out of his saddle, he hit ground, but still held the mule's rope.

The worst wasn't over, because the snake was still alive, and striking, as all three horses were prancing in panic, kicking every which way. Another hoof hit Tate in the chest, hurling him into the rattler. Reaching for a rock, Tate killed the snake with one crushing blow.

Then he fainted out cold.

# CHAPTER
## 8

RIGHT HERE, A LOT NEEDED HANDLING.

But, as I couldn't work everything all to once, I did the most important, nothing, while trying to decide what things to tackle, and in which order.

First, I hurried to my fallen brother.

Out cold. The snake was worse off. Well, old Tate wasn't going anywhere, and the mule (which I now needed) was headed for Georgia. The bay mare stood still, reins hanging. So I rode the buckskin, caught the mule, and hustled to our barn corral with all three animals. Dismounting, I rousted Gusher Plant and Slim Service, who were awake but not dressed, and told them to harness the mule and bring a small wagon, pronto, out beyond our ranch gate.

"What's doing?" Gusher wanted to know.

"Just handle it," I said. "I gotta go back and tend to my brother. He's down."

I changed horses, taking the bay mare, a horse less excitable than the buckskin gelding. At a full-out gallop I went back to where Tate Bodeen still lay on the ground next to a smashed rattlesnake. Kicking out of the saddle, I rushed to him, noticing his shirt in the early light. The cloth was cloudy with blood. My brother was either mashed unconscious or near to it.

The wagon arrived. Slim and Gusher came with it, jumped out, and started asking questions that we needed about as much as sand.

"What happened?" Slim asked, but the dead rattler answered it.

Carefully, we loaded Tate into the flatbed wagon, and carted him to the house. Mrs. Skagg didn't utter a word. She just fetched some shears and cut away Tate's shirt, peeling him like an onion. With a rag and hot water, she rinsed off the blood, then examined the two wounds with sensitive fingers.

"He busted ribs," she announced. "And it's more than just cracks. There's some loose ends. But I don't see any snake-fang punctures."

"The rattler's dead," I said.

Mrs. Skagg looked direct at me. "No matter. If your finger takes even a small prick or a scrape from the tip of a dead rattlesnake's fang, you'll maybe grant yourself a long visit to upstairs."

I was usual amazed as to how much Mrs. Skagg knew. Her brain was a schoolbook of useful stuff. One of my teachers, our library lady, was learned the same way. Her name was Miss Atherton, and she always about knew what I'd be looking for, where it was, and how to smoke it out.

Gusher and Slim continued to ask questions, mostly to each other, as neither of them were harvesting many replies from Mrs. Skagg or from me.

"Ribs," the old man said. "From the shape of his bruises, I reckon Tate must've blocked a hoof or two during the confusion over that cussed rattler."

"He'll be all right," Mrs. Skagg said, and the way she said it certain convinced me. Never had she ever lied to us. In fact, I doubted she'd ever told a story to anyone.

Using an old sheet, Mrs. Skagg cut it into long white strips, each bandage about four or five inches wide. With these she bound up Tate, around and around, whispering orders to Slim and Gusher to lift as she commanded. She wrapped him so tightly that I heard him groan. His face winced.

"There," she said. "Tate'll mend. But once we get him bedded, he's not to move unless the house is burning."

He was still in the wagon.

With two blankets and a pair of short poles, Slim contrived a stretcher, and then, with Gusher's assistance, carried Tate to his bedroom, to extend him out and cover him with a sheet.

"It's not serious," Mrs. Skagg confided in me, once the two of us were in the kitchen alone together. "Your brother's tougher than ox leather. Always has been. He's a chip off Mr. Sam Bodeen, so he'll be sound in a month. But he can't twitch or raise a fuss. If he does, we'll hogtie him to the bedposts, in a spread eagle."

Moving to the stove, she poured two mugs of coffee, one for herself and the other for me. We sat together at the kitchen table.

"Don't fret, Laddy." She touched my hand. "Your brother'll be sounding noise soon enough, shouting orders from his pillow. Seems like we got a spell to wait out." She winked at me. "Unless, of course, somebody can muster enough gumption to find those wild horses all by a lonesome and follow 'em back here to Kickaloo."

My mouth fell open.

"That's right," she told me. "Just maybe it might be Laddy Bodeen of the Buckle Tee cattle outfit."

My stomach rolled over. "Not me. When I threatened Tate that I'd go alone, I was only bluffing."

Her mouth was firmly set, lips tight. "I think it's high time you had yourself an enterprise. Can't conceive of a more golden chance. Nothing here to keep you. School's out."

I couldn't breathe. After a while, I asked her who would run the ranch with Tate down and me away somewhere. I wasn't, however, intending to go without Tate.

She snorted. "Same person who's run it, more or less, for years. *Me.* I just let Mr. Tate think he's doing it all. Plenty of times he asks me. Boy, do I tell him. Yet if I don't know the answer, I'll own up to that too, and the pair of us settle things out. Believe it or not, years back, I used to perform a similar function for another old horse hunter, your pa. Your mother didn't have a business head or a heart for ranching. Poems, yes . . . but not branding or castrating calves."

I winced.

Burning and cutting were two jobs I'd never taken to, either, or done well at, along with several of my other failures. All of which Tate had noticed with glances and thrashing words of disapproval. The thought of going after the horses certain sounded tempting. But to go without Tate . . .

"I'd be all alone out there," I said.

"Laddy, for years you been all alone right here to home. I know you"—she shot a glance over her shoulder—"better than I know that cookstove. You're a pea from her pod, youngster, like Sam Bodeen had nothing to do with your begetting. Tate is his. Not you. You were entirely of your mother's egg, her very own hatchling. And I'll tell you a surprise, son. It wasn't your mother who first noticed. Sam done it. Saw you touching flowers that grew close to the house, touching them with such gentleness. I stood there too. He looked at me, smiled, then pointed down at you, his little two-year-old, and said, 'This precious one is Lola May's.' "

"Papa said that?"

Mrs. Skagg nodded. "Indeed so. And because you were so much Lola May's child, your father would partial you to death. He'd favor you after that." Her eyes hardened. "Tate noticed it too. He saw his father leaving him, more than a mite, to add his special blessing to you, Laddy. No, it wasn't exactly what you could call easy on your brother's feelings. It buried under his hide worse'n a screw worm. Maybe that's how come Mr. Tate turned out to be the man he is. Who knows? Certainly not an old stork of a woman who curses hot words at a cold stove."

I couldn't imagine I was hearing all of these things. Yet I believed it all, because Mrs. Skagg was telling me.

"She was lonely, like you," she said.

"My mother?"

"Yes. Toward the end, before that dreadful happening, your mother used to stroll off by herself, singing to clouds. T'was her mind leaving too. Although it isn't very Christian to speak it out, perhaps it was a blessing that day. That red roan gelding maybe knew what terminal act of mercy had to be done."

My body began to tremble. Hearing what Mrs. Skagg was saying was a lot like the rodeo last Sunday, and hearing the raging of bulls and broncs and calves in their fright. Perhaps, in her own secret way, my mother had been bellowing too, only her cry of fear was silent.

"Quite so." Mrs. Skagg went to the stove for more coffee from the pot, and then returned to the table. "You're a loner too, Laddy, as she was. So you might as well try to make the loneliness work to your favor. Apply it like soap against stain. Go fetch those horses home."

"To be honest, I'm scared to try."

She nodded. "Of course you're sore afraid. It comes with the territory. Rough country. As frightening as having to face a new idea." She took a breath. "But you'd better give it a whirl, on account if you don't, you'll never bust free of your brother. Freedom isn't given, boy. It's taken. Grabbed. Often snatched from one fist to another."

Without another word, she left the kitchen and I heard her in Papa's room. She was gone for over five minutes but then returned, a yellowing piece of paper in her hand. "If you ever doubt," she said, "that I know what's going on around the Buckle Tee, you'd best give yourself a second guess. Fact of the matter is, I been thinking a bit about Dodge Yardell myself lately . . . on how much I'd like you and Tate to know him, while he's still standing."

Sitting down, she opened up the paper and we studied it together. It was a map. At the upper end of the paper, the north end, was Kickaloo, our hometown. And down at the bottom of the sheet, the south end, I saw an *X* marking a spot, and a name crudely printed.

*Yardell.*

As Mrs. Skagg's red shiny hands searched the paper, she complained that she couldn't see too well without glasses, and asked me to translate the fine print. A series of circles ran south. What they meant, however, was a mystery.

"These circles," I asked, "what are they?"

"Water towers. They'll be your landmarkers on the trip south. Take a compass. Your best bet is to find Mr. Dodge Yardell first thing you do. Your pa used to claim that nobody on earth could recite poetry to horses like his friend."

"When do I start?" Knowing that I might convince Mr. Yardell to help made me feel sudden braver.

Mrs. Skagg stood up quickly. "This morning. You can't think too much about a dentist. Go sit in his chair and open your mouth. It's the only way I know to get rid of a sorry tooth and lick the cusser."

I stood up too, on wobbling knees.

"Get going," she told me, "before your grit quits." She handed me the refolded map.

"Thanks for telling me all about my folks, and about Tate as well, and Dodge Yardell."

"Forget it. Tell old Gusher Plant to reload that mule for you, and watch him do it. In fact, do it yourself and allow him to teach you. Gush is a windbag, but he does more'n a few things correct and always has. He's solid."

"Okay, I will."

I sort of stood still.

"Well . . . get a wiggle on," she said.

Somehow, I couldn't move. All I could do was suspect that I'd forgotten to do something really important, with an old woman who had so suddenly become so special to me.

"And," she said sternly, "Slim or Gusher might insist on going along with you, but you tell 'em *no*. They're both to keep to home and chores if they expect to fill their bellies off *my* stove. And with Tate down, I'll need the both of them."

"So long," I told her. My voice sounded more than a bit sorrowful as I was saying it. And on top of that, my boots couldn't seem to move.

Mrs. Skagg understood. Opening her lean arms, she held them out to me, and I gave her a hug. She smelled like breakfast, soap, and hard work.

"There," she said, "now git south."

BOOK

TWO

# CHAPTER
## 9

DUE SOUTH.

Underneath me trotted a bay mare. She was a rich blackstrap brown, with a black mane and tail, and Tate said that she could burden a man to Perdition and back in one day.

"I've decided to give you a name," I told her, "because my brother never would. From now on, your name is Brownie because you're so doggone sweet-natured."

Behind me, the mule hee-hawed, sawing through the July morning air with an abrasive braying.

"Evelyn," I said, "you're sweet too."

As I was leaving our ranch, Gusher Plant had told me that if I got myself hopeless lost, I was to give Evelyn her head, whack her backside, and then follow her north. All the way home to the Buckle Tee. "That mule," Gusher had claimed, "could educate pigeons."

When the sun was high, about noon, I stopped off under some spreading-oak shade to rest all three of us, to gnaw a carrot and some dried beef, and to check the diamond-back lashing on Evelyn's load. She wasn't hauling real heavy. Just a tent and poles, rope, foodstuffs, and a good supply of clean clothes, including a

rain slicker and a Buckle Tee branding iron in full view. The iron
had been Slim's idea, so that I could brand any captured horses
right away and burn in our legal claim.

Overhead, a circling hawk screamed its two-noter, announcing
its hunger to Heaven.

"Well now, ladies," I said to the mule and my bay horse, "best
we continue." Checking her cinch, I mounted Brownie and
neck-reined her due south. My mare was an eager little horse,
happy perhaps that she carried so light a rider, and she stepped
out perky as a fan dancer.

"Good gal," I told her, "good Brownie."

I patted her neck so she could feel and hear my approval of
her willingness. To touch Sue Louise Hartberry would be a mite
more fun. As I rode, her name and face were ringing inside me
like a nobody-home telephone. I didn't really like Sue Louise. All
I did was love her, from a safe distance.

The afternoon wore on.

In my shirt pockets I discovered two of Mrs. Skagg's buttermilk biscuits and ate both of them. Coming to a patch of really
good thick grass I let my two animals graze for what I determined was about half an hour. In among the grass, I spotted the
long willowy tops of wild onions, so I uprooted a handful, and
boiled them over a small fire.

"These are really not bad," I said, adding salt for a smack of
flavor.

I contributed some wild onions to my left saddlebag, in case
my food ran short as I ventured further south.

How far was it to Republic Flat? That was a question I
couldn't answer rightly. Only guess at. Papa's wore-out map
didn't exactly say, or even hint. Perhaps it was possible that Tate
knew, yet he had been in no condition to explain anything, or
even tell us what his name was.

Right about now, I imagined, Tate Bodeen had regained full consciousness and was demanding food, drink, and a plug of his Red Man chewing tobacco. I had a hunch that Mrs. Skagg would service his requests at her own pace, as if she were some eccentric old auntie.

Come to think about it, I couldn't ever remember a time that Gusher and Mrs. Skagg weren't working at the Buckle Tee. Our outfit was their home, their only home, and I reckon that both of them knew certain that neither Tate nor I would ever turn them out. Mrs. Skagg continued to earn her keep as a cook and housekeeper, and as (I had recently learned) an adviser to my brother. Before that, to my father. As for Gusher Plant, he had been a part of our cattle business even before Mrs. Skagg. As far as I was concerned, when their time came, both Gusher and Mrs. Skagg ought to be allowed the dignity of death among us, plus the honor, well-earned, of being buried on the knoll in our family plot, beside Mama.

My daddy would lie there too, someday. Not yet. Because I wasn't ready to give him up, even though everyone else at the Buckle Tee had.

Riding south, I kept remembering the spark of interest that I saw on Papa's face, and in his eyes, when I'd mentioned that Tate and I were going to try to capture the mustangs. At the word *horses,* his face brightened. Yes, there might be hope for Sam Bodeen. It would require more patience, and time, and perhaps some little spur of recollection, a jab of memory pricking into his shadowy world, a secret light.

The mule brayed.

"Evelyn," I said, "there's nothing wrong. You just follow along. Hear?" My hand tightened on the rope that was leading her.

There was no sense stopping until sundown. So I kept heading south, with the evening sun now setting slightly behind my right shoulder. It stopped being a bright golden star and softened to a crimson wafer. In a sense, there was something holy about it, something to help battle fear, and it gave me a feeling of closeness to the western sky.

"Hey, look over yonder at that pretty sunset, you animals," I said to Evelyn and Brownie.

They wouldn't oblige me. So I turned all of us to the west, realizing how Tate would mutter, were he here, and question my sanity. It wouldn't be Tate Bodeen's style to display a Florida sundown to a mule. Pearls before swine? Yet who could honestly attest that animals can't appreciate beauty? Gusher once said that he'd seen a mockingbird actual trim the rim of a nest with a flower. But who could be such a simpleton as to believe an old waddy like Gusher Plant? Gush, as we all knew, had a way of saying more than his prayers.

"No doubt about it, ladies," I said, "our day is just about wore itself down to quit."

Night was falling.

We stopped, even though I had sort of counted on spotting the first of the water towers prior to sundown, and I pulled off Brownie's saddle and Evelyn's pack.

Using the saddle blanket, I rubbed each animal briskly, until the damp sweat had disappeared off their backs and they lightened to an original dry. Making a fire, I boiled some beans, a cautious portion because I was still a bit fearful of running out of grub or canteen water. There was a slim possibility that we could live on wild onions and grazing grass. However, I would do whatever was necessary to find Mr. Dodge Yardell; then, if possible, the loose band of horses.

"Ladies," I said, "I don't really want to tether you, or hobble you, but we can't take a chance on your leaving during the night. Can we?"

No answer.

Evelyn just looked at me, the way only a mule can study a fool. Brownie merely nickered a quiet whinny and then was still.

"So," I said, "I'll just hobble you both a bit, so you won't be tempted to stray off."

I pitched the tent. It covered a very modest amount of ground, and inside I had to curl myself up into a ball in order to keep completely within the flaps.

An owl screamed.

Perhaps the owl was perturbed that three large beings came to frighten the prey and to send them scurrying underground, away from the talons of hunger. The ground felt so hard. Several times, I'd been camping out with Gusher, so I wasn't feeling as though I was experiencing the unfamiliar. Yet it was night, I was alone and a long way from the Buckle Tee ranch. I'd slept alone before, but only out in our meadow on Bodeen property. Here, I didn't know who owned the property, if anyone, or what tomorrow would bestow.

"Mrs. Skagg," I said to the night, "you were right. I really am alone here."

In a matter of minutes, complete blackness fell like a hammer on the anvil of unyielding earth, a big black pounding of fright that seemed to beat me into ground like a tent peg.

"Now," I said almost aloud, "the moment has come to decide whether or not I am a coward. This tonight is going to be the hardest. My initial test."

My jaw trembled.

The first night would prove to be a lot longer than eight seconds on a rodeo bull. And yet those seconds had been one painful eternity, more than my crotch could endure. I'd secretly decided that bull riders and bronc riders had to be eunuchs. Why, I was wondering, was castration always around wherever mankind prowled? Hold it, my mind warned. That wasn't exactly true. Gusher Plant had once said that gray squirrels and red squirrels were bitter enemies, but the reds were far more ferocious, and would bite off the balls of the gray males.

Balls.

It was one of Tate Bodeen's favorite words, especially when referring to a kid brother who couldn't handle the ranch work, or stick on a rodeo bull all the way to a buzzer.

Half-asleep, I thought about Sue Louise Hartberry, and how I wanted to own a motorcycle and be Bill Tarky, feeling the warm closeness of Sue Louise against my spine. Oh, I would cuddle a feeling like that. I could eat it. Worship it. Sue Louise knew she'd be a cheerleader even when she was only twelve years old. And now, at age fourteen, she was the hottest flapper in town. She knew it, and so did every male.

"Hey," I said aloud, "if I keep thinking about Sue Louise's legs, and how she rolls the tops of her stockings, I won't be afraid of the dark."

Maybe, I was thinking, this is the prime gift that women give men. They keep them courageous. When a guy is alone in a tent, all he has to do is remember Sue Louise Hartberry, the forbidden dessert, prepared in Hell's pantry to drive boys crazy.

"Sue Louise," I said in my deepest voice, "I have come for you, my girl." Yes, to carry you away on my motorcycle to some faraway kingdom, there to gnaw your knees. I was falling asleep, yet the fantasy was too vivid to release, too delicious, too . . . *Sue Louise!*

When I moved my leg, my right ankle ached like blazes where the rodeo bull had stomped me. I wondered if it was busted.

Outside my tiny shelter, Brownie fluttered a nasal good night.

Not loud. Merely a suggestion that she was nearby, a part of the Buckle Tee that had come along with me, to sustain my quest. My hip hurt. Florida seemed to harden as the night thickened. I wasn't quite yet asleep.

Drowsy only.

"So," I said, "maybe we all ought to close our eyes. . . ." I couldn't force myself to do it, because whenever my eyelids would sag, I'd fight them open again, because it was night. And I was really alone. My fingernails clawed into the sandy soil so I wouldn't panic and head back home, in retreat.

*Home,* what a warming word. Half-asleep, I was hoping that somebody would see that my father was all right. And had his light blanket to hold. This was my nightly habit, back home, and it wasn't a chore or a duty.

"Good night, Papa."

Slowly, I relaxed against the hard ground, melting, becoming a part of it, blending with all the quiet Florida night which became a nest, a cradle, and took me inside her arms like a mother I once had.

And lost.

# CHAPTER
## 10

GRACKLES.

Grackles woke me.

Poking my head out of the small tent, I squinted into a fog that dawn was trying to chase away.

About a hundred black grackles were gathered nearby, strutting on the damp grass, engaged in a breakfast argument. For several seconds, I watched their minstrel show, listening to the abrasive sounds of their debate. One nearby bird looked at me with his yellow eye, as if resenting my invasion of his territory. As I pushed open the tent flap, the grackles screamed a chorus and took off. Black blots melted into a gray sky.

My mare and mule had not strayed far.

"Good morning, ladies," I said.

While crawling out of the little shelter, my body felt more than a bit stiff. Good old Crankshaft. That black bull had nailed agony all over me, in layers, overlapping like shingles. It was difficult to determine where one cramp left off to greet another. Limping about twenty feet away from my tent, I stood in a tall patch of green weeds and emptied myself. I sighed. All around me, the weedy stalks stretched upward, then spread out into extended fingers, reminding me of a classroom of young children, hands raised, ready with an answer to the question of a fresh day.

A question indeed.

"Well," I said aloud, "I best get my team tacked and going. Republic Flat, here we come."

Still hobbled, the mare and mule were both grazing, lifting their heads alternately to munch as if each one were standing guard for the other. Or for me.

A July morning comes early in Florida.

Before I'd finished my biscuits, topped off with a handful of prunes, the sun invaded the fog and sparkled the dew. Finding a low hole filled with black water, I let the animals drink. Then, with a trusting shrug, I boiled some of it for coffee. By itself, in its natural state, the water wouldn't have been too tasty. In the past, I'd tried to drink pasture water one time, and only once. Better drinking could be drained out of a truck radiator.

My mule was grazing alarmingly close to the weeds. Grass I trusted, but Florida is peppered with rattleweed, and it doesn't take too ample a serving to turn a horse or a cow into a runamuck. Hurriedly, I led Evelyn back to the short grass. A breeze kicked up, carding the taller grass as if it were a giant pelt of green hair.

The grass rippled like water.

While saddling the mare, I sure had a hanker to hear old Gusher Plant's harmonica, or to listen up to Slim's singing. Slim Service would often wander from the bunkhouse to the main house, coming for breakfast, and singing . . . "Oh, the thumb of God be emerald green, He called it Floriday."

"Be still," Gusher would sometimes complain to his workmate. "It's morning, so let the Lord wake up in peace, and me too."

Slim, to stand up for his rights, once told Gusher, "You sure can throw a pile of talk."

Evelyn gave out a griping hee-haw about the pack, kicked, then accepted her burden, following Brownie and me willingly behind a sagging rope. I looped the free end around the saddle horn to ease my raw hand, which still burned from yesterday. The compass arrowed me south. It was all I could do to keep from bolting north, toward home, at a gallop.

My whole face forced a grin when, after about two hours, I spotted the first water tower.

"Ladies," I said, "we're on trail."

Riding closer told me that the water tower hadn't held any water for a good many years. Nor could it. Several of the vertical staves were missing. Black gaps separated the graying boards, and the iron rings were rusted to a dusty brown. Top to bottom, I guessed that the water tower wasn't more than twenty feet tall. Leaving it, I wondered who had built it here, and why. Some sturdy dreamer, perhaps, who figured he could somehow do battle with Florida sun and wind, and figured wrong.

South of the tower stood one ancient orange tree, its upper branches buckhorned into lifeless stubs. Below, the sour-root greenery was still alive but not thriving. I saw one pathetic orange hanging from a stem. Riding to it, I felt it more out of curiosity than desire. The little brown orange was hard, dry, and had perhaps lingered on the tree as some mysterious warning to future growers. *Don't try it here.*

We pushed south.

Ahead, vegetation thickened, dictating that our direct southern route was no longer possible. I began to serpentine my horse and mule, circling first eastward then to the west, to avoid the patches of damp earth and heavy mud. When we came to the swamp, it seemed to stretch limitlessly to my left and right, impossible to avoid. Unfolding the map Mrs. Skagg had given me proved of little help. On the paper, there was no swamp. Yet here it was, confronting, confounding, wild and green and menacing, a vast black mirror of silent water.

"Girls," I said, "we're wading through."

Right then, I was feeling too impatient to fritter all day searching for a way around the swamp, not when there were mustangs to be hunted.

Brownie, my little mare, did not want to go. She knew, perhaps, that she was a dry-land animal and not a mudder. Her ears flattened for the first time. It took several kicks and some coaxing to urge her hoofs into their first splash.

The black muck sucked on every hoof, creating a wet oozing noise when a hoof was lifted, as if the swamp was trying to claim us for its own. Fan palms sprouted up everywhere, their stems bristling with mean rows of hooking thorns.

Yesterday, the trees I'd ridden past were thin scrubby oaks, flocks of them, and the taller cabbage palms and stands of pines, pines, pines. But here in the swamp I saw cypress, red maple, fig, and a giant gumbo-limbo tree. On a tiny patch of high ground, a scorpion crouched on what looked like wet limestone dust. Sounds changed. Here there seemed to be no crows, woodpeckers, wrens, or sparrows. Birds here were wading birds, standing sometimes on one long and slender leg. I saw a white ibis; then heard an anhinga, a water turkey, and saw her spreading her black wings to dry on the leafless trunk of a dead bell-bottom cypress.

The mare saw the bird move, and reacted as though to bolt.

"Easy," I said.

Frogs and cicadas became louder, more numerous. A flash— and a frog would never croak again. The slashing rapier beak of a giant blue-gray heron ended his concert. Beak straight up like a church spire, the heron swallowed the frog whole. Still kicking in death, the frog created a futile falling lump inside the long slender gullet.

Brownie stepped into a deeper slough, sinking quickly to her chest, nickering in fear, kicking, splashing. Black water and blacker mud were spattering all over us. Her back arched as if cocking her body to buck.

With the reins, I picked up her head. "Steady now," I told her. "We'll get through." I backed her, and we tried an alternate route, crashing through the vine-tangled jungle. My wincing face moved through the large sticky web of a hairy wolf spider. "Keep on," I told Brownie whenever she'd balk.

To my right, a light-colored pine snake weaved its way along the surface of the black water, coming our way. Seeing us, the snake paused, the fork of its tongue testing the air to absorb information. Then it retreated.

"Okay," I kept telling my two animals. "It's going to be okay, because this swamp isn't even on our map, so it can't go on forever."

All around, green ferns grew taller than any other ferns I'd ever seen. All lace, several looking a lot like cypress greenery. The air was thicker too, like porridge, heavy and damp and clinging. Fungus, vines, moss abounded, along with insects, gnats, and chiggers. I had to jump Brownie over a fallen log that lay rotting in the pungent water. A bug bit my neck and I slapped it, frightening the mare. She plunged into soft earth, then water, back to earth again where I halted her.

"Brownie, old girl, we can't panic in here or raise up a fuss. Slow and steady now. We'll handle it. Let's go."

Like the willing little mount she was, my mare responded to the touch of my heels. Mounds of moss, round as emerald breasts, seemed to flourish on the spines of half-submerged logs and fallen trees. These smaller logs the mare stepped over, others had to be skirted and avoided.

A male wood duck, showing off his rainbow of plumage, darted through a stand of tawny cattails.

"I can smell wild coffee," I told my horse. "That and muscadine berries. And watch out for those hornets, Brownie."

As her hoofs stirred up the murky water, fingerlings of bass and bream swarmed frantically to attack the disturbed mosquito larvae, darting their sleek and silvery hulls through the small clouds of aroused silt. Tendrils of hydrilla weed clutched and clung to the twigs of low-growing trees.

A tiny green tree frog quacked five times, ducklike, and then resumed his earlier silence.

Had I not been so wary of the sloughs of swamp water, I would have admired the eerie beauty of the place. Filtering down through the lace of the high cypress fell prisms of sunshine, tiny shards and fragments of light that danced as the overhead cypress boughs swayed. My horse and my mule, however, were obviously unhappy. They wanted to get out by the shortest and quickest possible route.

Again and again, the mule's lead rope scorched my hand. The burning was advancing from a mere discomfort into a steady pain.

"Come along, Evelyn," I kept saying to her.

My encouragement amounted to little use. The mule just plain hated where she was, yet, in a number of instances, refused to leave where she was standing. "Nobody," according to the wisdom of one Gusher Plant, "can truly understand a mule's brain. Not even," he went on to say, "another mule, like Tate Bodeen."

Ahead, there seemed to be no end to the swamp. No promise of a clearing or a lessening of all the greenery and undergrowth. Several times, I was tempted to turn around and go back, yet I didn't exactly know where I'd been or which way I had come. It sure was one confusing place. My body flinched at the worry of wondering how big the swamp really was, and the nag of having to be in there all day. And all *night,* a time in a swamp that could prove dismal enough to scare God.

"Move," I told Brownie. "We're almost out."

It was a boldface lie. Because I certain didn't know any more than the gnat that was chewing on the back of my neck. I swatted it. But I had at least found some dryer land and had convinced the two animals to stay on it until I could figure which way was forward, south, and which avenue would lead us into the clear.

A flock of birds, which I couldn't see clearly as they were overhead in the cypress lace, began to chirp away in a scolding fashion. To my ear, it sounded like some sort of a warning, and maybe those chattering cousins were disturbed about something that I didn't know.

The sudden *hiss* about froze my heart.

It came from behind me. Glancing backward, I noticed the mule's white eyes rolling in fright, and as she bolted, the rope whipped out of my raw hand.

Then I saw the gator.

# CHAPTER
## 11

THE MULE KNEW.

For some unknown reason, I hollered out, "Gator!" but my yelling wasn't needed or heeded. Evelyn had sensed it before I did. So had the heckling birds.

The alligator was about thirty or forty feet away, off to our right, and behind us. All I could see was a very black lagoon of deep water, and the *snout*. That big blunt head, nose forward, cutting a V-wake along the surface of the water.

"Evelyn!"

Spurring the mare, I tried to lean down and make a grab at the loose rope, but it snaked away. The mule was thrashing in the deep water, churning up mud but going really nowhere. It was like I saw one of my own nightmares where somebody evil is pursuing me and my feet are embedded in glue. But now, the mule's hoofs were living such a horror.

I was yelling.

"Evelyn! Evelyn!"

Meanwhile, my mare had now wheeled and saw the approaching predator. On dry land, this would have presented no problem for Brownie, but here, circumstances were different. Shaking her head, ears back against the crest of her mane, the mare fought the bit. Again and again the reins were nearly torn from my left hand.

Brownie bucked.

Memories of the past Sunday rushed into my mind, and I was again astride an angry Galloway bull. I was high in the air with a crazed animal between my legs, battling a swamp and a monster that was about to attack us. But this was no Kickaloo Junior Rodeo, no band playing its brassy razzmatazz, and today was more important than eight seconds and a fake-silver belt buckle.

"Whoa . . . Brownie, whoa."

My eyes darted from the mule to the gator. He was closer now, coming steadily, with the unhurried confident advance of a chess player who knows the enemy army is confined, in trouble, and ripe for a slaughter.

The mare was rearing, kicking up water and wet muck, struggling against the reins, ears flat, fighting the bit and the bridle. It was the mule who stood between us and the gator. Our wild-eyed mule whose name was Evelyn and who never had been in a swamp.

Leaning over once again, my hand stretched down to snare Evelyn's rope.

It was there. All I had to do was clutch it and then spur Brownie away, and save the mule. So simple. And so impossible.

"Evelyn!"

The mule became a gray granite statue. Standing in knee-deep water, she ceased her thrashing as she seemingly could do nothing now except stare at the knobby wet head. The gator's jaws were still closed. Yet it came. Closer. And closer. Then the yellow eyes flashed in anticipation and the great jaws parted slightly, fangs exposed.

I tried to spur the mare toward the gator, to crush its skull with the superior weight of a quarterhorse's hoofs. It was possible. The smashing power of one hoof of a horse is crushing, regardless of whether the horse is striking with a forehoof or kicking with a rear one. And the teeth. Any beast who underestimates the jaw strength of a horse is an imbecile.

Even a child's pet pony has a bite worse than a plumber's pliers.

The mule brayed in panic.

"Evelyn!"

Leaping up and out of the water, the gator showed his creamy-white underbelly, and all those jagged scales of rawhide armor. Jaws fully open, he hissed.

The mule knew.

I heard her fright.

Then, a second later, the swamp water turned from a cold, murky black to red. A steamy red. Blood red. All I could do was try to remain in the saddle, on Brownie, who by now had become one hysterical animal.

Again, I heard the *hiss.*

Yesterday, I had heard the buzz of a rattlesnake. No comparing. A gator's hiss, from an attacking alligator in a swamp, has to be one of the most petrifying warnings ever to invade a victim's ear, regardless of whether such ear is bestial or human. The hiss is a sound that cuts, it whips like a snake, to saw through one's sanity and cudgel all reason.

"Run . . . Evelyn, run!"

It was over in a matter of seconds.

In a breath, the swamp water was boiling, churning, with bubbles rising from everywhere. After an instant, I had no mule. Only a pool of flesh, tissue, bone, and a memory of her service to the Buckle Tee. Close to a thousand hauling trips into Kick-aloo and a thousand trips home.

Ended.

Wide-eyed, I saw the gator swim away, its tail thrashing, its jaws gripping part of an animal I once knew. The mule's body had been cut in half. Divided. Jaws too vicious to describe had clamped into a docile gray animal and won.

The water stilled.

I smelled blood everywhere, and the sickly sweet stench of it made me gag. From all I could see, as I tried to control a rearing mare, what little remained was a leg and a head, and blood, blood, blood. Quietly, slowly, the pack floated up and out of the murky water. Stretching down, I grabbed a rope and the handle of the branding iron and then hauled it close to me.

Moving as if in a trance, the mare and I somehow found our way out of the swamp with the help of my compass, and once again onto dry earth and into sunshine.

I dragged part of the mule's pack.

"Whoa," I said.

Brownie would not come to a stand. She continued to prance, moving sideways, spinning around in dizzying circles as though to check what was behind her. Her action prevented me from dismounting. My hand still held the pack by its rope, but my grip couldn't last, so I let loose. I'd been more dragging the pack than toting it.

My left eye was smarting because so much mucky dirt and water had splattered up.

It made little sense, yet I kept saying our mule's name over and over. "Evelyn . . . Evelyn . . . Evelyn . . ." She was gone, torn apart, as I could do nothing more than watch it happen, and holler. Blood was on the mare, and on me, but I wasn't at all certain whose blood it was. Mine? The mare's? The dead mule's? I gagged. Even with my eyes closed, I could see it happening again, hear it, and smell the odor of gushing blood.

In a wide easy circle, I trotted the mare around the damaged and mud-caked pack, thankful I'd at least saved that, and the

Buckle Tee branding iron. Over and over, I talked to my horse, trying to settle her. Finally it worked. Her trot became more disciplined, more even, her ears perked up, and she quit tossing her head and cribbing on the bit. She was sucking in air though, breathing unevenly, and so was I. Time and again, still riding her in circles, my mind saw the gator ripping into our mule.

"Go slow, Brownie," I said.

Gradually, I calmed her trot into a walk, around and around the pack that centered our circle upon the sand. My eyes couldn't help looking at it, as part of her pack was all I had left of poor old Evelyn. She was a good animal, had pulled hard, and she deserved a better death. Nevertheless, it was over now, but the tragedy of losing the mule was only beginning to dawn on me. Glancing at my damaged provisions, I knew that I'd best do some deciding on what stuff to take and which to leave behind.

I dismounted, then hobbled the mare in some solitary oak shade and sat, leaning my backbone against the tree trunk.

"Brownie," I said, "maybe we ought to turn back while you and I still got each other."

With my spine pressing against the hardness of the tree, eyes closed, I could think of nothing except losing the mule. Her fear and pain kept braying into my ears, again and again, spikes of guilt that continued to stab into my brain. Evelyn's death wasn't her fault. Or even the gator's. It was mine. Entirely mine. This horse hunt was my quest, not hers.

"Gator," I whispered in private, "you should've taken *me,* not my mule."

Evelyn . . . Evelyn . . .

Her name seemed to repeat itself inside my conscience, hauntingly, as if tormenting me that I'd been so foolhardy as to risk two good animals as well as myself.

Surely there had to have been a route around the swamp. Yet, in my eagerness to capture a band of mustangs, I had plunged forward, chasing wild horses as though they were wild geese. I hadn't seen any horses. I'd only heard some hearsay in a feed store back north in Kickaloo, from a man who himself hadn't seen the horses either, and maybe never would.

For this, some crazy kid's dream of quick money and instant manhood, the kid had killed a trusty old ranch animal. How old had Evelyn been? In all my years, I couldn't ever recall a time on the Buckle Tee without our mule. She was always there. Always pulling, giving a full day's sweat whenever it was asked of her, and that was constantly.

"Ladd Bodeen," I said, "you're not only a coward. You are also the dumbest kind of fool."

Lifting my head, I looked north. Perhaps the mule's being killed was a sign, a warning, telling me to turn back while there was still a Brownie.

Still a me.

# CHAPTER
## 12

"THERE IT IS," I SAID.

Brownie twitched an ear, not knowing that I had sighted the second water tower. The compass had helped more than a bit.

Earlier, I had sorted through the pack that the mule had been burdening, saved some things, discarding others, which I made sure to bury. It made no sense at all to leave a trail that an idiot could follow. I didn't want anyone to know who I was, why I was here, or which direction I headed.

"Brownie," I said as we passed by the water tower, "we're on our way to an enterprise."

In my attempt to deepen my voice, to sound more manly and reassuring to the mare, I probable sounded somewhat like a circus clown. No matter. Mile by mile, I was gradual recovering from the shock of losing Evelyn to the alligator. I wasn't over it, nor would I ever be, as the experience was too jolting. On top of that, I'd have some fancy explaining due Tate when I got home, concerning our mule.

It was about nearing late afternoon.

Ahead, I spotted a strange sight. Above the pines and cabbage palms, I saw what appeared to be a very thin spire of smoke. My guess was not a campfire. Rather, a chimney. Riding closer, I could then see that I'd been correct. A small shack, in rather a pitiful condition, sat among a tall stand of pines. A few chickens pecked the dirt by the dooryard.

Should I stop?

Before I could answer my own question, the door opened and a girl emerged, carrying what appeared to be a bundle of clothes. Brownie neighed a fluttering salutation that caused the girl to look my way, wide-eyed and startled.

"Howdy!" I yelled.

She froze.

"My name's Laddy Bodeen and I'm from back north, up in Kickaloo. Our outfit is called the Buckle Tee." As I made the statement, I pulled my  **BT**  branding iron from behind my saddle and waved it like a baton. The girl disappeared inside the cabin, but then reappeared quicker than a blink, but not empty-handed. Instead of a bundle of cloth, or whatever it was, she now held a shotgun.

"Hold it right there," she said, as the shotgun's black hole was leveling at my head.

"Hey," I said, "please don't shoot. I'm not an enemy or anything. I'm Laddy Bodeen."

"So you say. You just sit there righteous, or maybe your head'll slow a lead berry. What's worse, I know how to shoot a man where it hurts the most."

The girl looked to be about my age, or younger. She was fragile and pale, with hair the color of corn, a soft yellow. The sunlight invited her hair to dance.

I grinned. "What's your name?"

"Never mind," she told me. But I noticed that the muzzle of her shotgun was lowering a friendly inch. "Mister, you best lighten your horse."

"What?"

"Fall off and sit," she said. "You look harmless."

"Well, I'm not. I happen to be a right dangerous criminal, as anybody'll clear see."

The girl grunted. "You don't got a mean freckle on your face. If'n you want to take a look at mean, you ought to see the man whose cabin this is. His name is Bad Murphy . . . and he'd snatch a bone from a bear-dog. So mind your manners."

I dismounted slowly.

"What are you doing along here?" she asked.

"Well," I said, taking a cautious step toward her and the gray board shack behind her, "I was sort of wondering if you could maybe point me toward a place called Republic Flat."

She spat.

"Don't budge a damn inch," she said. "You're on it." I laughed. "My name's Cora. My full name is Cora Emily Blike, and I forgot what you said how you like to be called."

"Ladd Bodeen."

"You got any liquor?"

"Me?"

"I ain't asking your horse."

"No, not a drop."

Her question reminded me that I was only fifteen and in my entire life hadn't tasted even the first drop of strong spirits. I studied Cora Blike. She was rough but pretty, the sort of a girl who could collect your total attention quicker than a toothache.

"I got some food," I told her.

"So have I. Maybe we can swap a munch of yours for a munch of mine, and round out supper."

I nodded. "Suits me, Cora."

She rested the shotgun near the door. "Bad Murphy'll be coming home soon, so watch yourself around me. He's terrible jealous. A doggone animal, that man. If'n he as much as suspects you trespass me, he'll fry your liver and feed it to the chickens."

I gulped.

"Golly," I said, "I haven't ever started to trespass on anyone. I didn't come to stir trouble, I'm just passing by."

Cora nodded to a bucket. "You want to wash? There's so much scurf near you, maybe you'll need a shovel to lift it off. And there's more burrs on your shirt than there be on three stray dogs. Where'd you get so dirt filthy?"

I pointed north.

"Back in the swamp, the one just south of the first water tower I came to. I'd started out with a mule as a pack animal, but a gator killed her."

"They'll do such," Cora sighed. "As I gather it, trouble usual comes in two sizes. Slow and quick. If'n you're ready and prepared, it'll arrive slow. But when a person ain't cocked or loaded, trouble's got a way of swooping down like a owl."

Using a rusty relic of a knife, Cora cut a ring around the hind legs of a dead gray squirrel, slit its belly from crotch to throat, then cut off its tail. With one motion, she yanked both rear legs to skin the squirrel; whacked off all four paws, and gutted it. It took less than a minute.

Later, I offered her dried plums. To even it out, Cora served us a tin plate of hot squirrel meat. We ate astride a log in front of her shack. She'd also boiled a few wild turnip roots.

"Back home," I told her, "we feed turnips to hogs."

"So do I," Cora said. "Help yourself."

She certain had a fair portion of humor.

In between bites of grub, Cora looked at me with eyes that seemed to have invented the color of blue. She sure was a looker. At first, I hadn't thought so, on account she had been standing behind that big shotgun that belonged to the man she lived with,

Bad Murphy. Yet the more I looked at Cora Blike in her flour-sack dress and bare feet, chewing squirrel meat, the prettier she bloomed.

I offered her another of my dried plums, or prunes, as Mrs. Skagg calls them.

"These taste all-right good," she said.

I couldn't help wondering if Bad Murphy was fixing to show up soon. Anyhow, if he did, I don't guess I'd given him any cause for distress. Nobody could get too ornery over a prune . . . unless somebody's first name was Bad. When I heard the next unmistakable sound, I near about choked on a prune pit. Then I looked at Cora to ask one of the stupidest questions a boy could ask a girl. "What was that?"

Shaking her head, as if dealing with an imbecile, Cora explained the noise. *"That . . . is my baby."*

I held my breath for an instant. "How did you get a baby?"

Cora laughed. "The usual way."

So *that* was the bundle that Cora Blike had been carrying when I first saw her. A baby. Without another word, Cora went into the cabin and then returned to the log we were sitting on.

"His name's Burlin."

My face wouldn't quite perform a smile. And then my lower jaw dropped nearly to my chest when Cora handed the baby to me. He wasn't very big. Or heavy. With my hands encircling his middle, my thumbs almost touching across his chest, I held little Burlin as far from me as I could stretch. Burlin was yelping fit to kill, and kicking his little pink feet.

"He won't bite," Cora said. "So you don't have to keep him at arm's length like an old man holds a hymnbook. Cradle him some. Tuck him up tight against your neck and shoulder. He ain't a skunk. He's my child, and he's sweet as taffy."

As she suggested, I carefully drew Burlin close to me and

cuddled my arms around him. He still bleated aplenty. But at least he quit kicking.

"He won't seem to turn quiet," I said. "Maybe Burlin's not feeling so good. Is he sickly?"

The girl smiled.

"Shucks, no, he ain't sick. I don't guess you know even a speck about baby tending. Burlin's just hungry."

"Oh. Are you going to give him a bottle of milk?" Looking around, I didn't see a cow anywhere. Or a goat. There certain was no store out here in the flat and lonely. "But," I said, "you don't keep a cow."

Cora giggled.

Taking her baby from me, she sat and held him in one arm, using a free hand to open the top of her raggy dress. I couldn't breathe. Even though I was trying to be a gentleman and not stare, I couldn't help looking at Cora's breast. I don't guess I'd ever had the honor of seeing anything so delightful to look at. I wanted to touch her. Before I could move or think or take my next breath, Burlin's face covered the nipple. One of his hands clutched at her breast flesh as he began to suck his mother's milk. I'd never seen a girl undressed before. Or even kissed one.

Plenty of times I'd thought about kissing Sue Louise Hartberry, but I wasn't considering it now.

The girl wasn't looking at me. Instead, she looked down at her nursing child, then lowered her chin until it touched the little boy's head. I don't guess I'd ever seen so graceful a gesture. It was more music than motion. And I wasn't at all surprised when I heard Cora begin to hum. Whatever song it was, I didn't recognize its title. Low, sweet, softer than fleece.

It made me forget all about hunting horses.

All I could wonder about was whether my own mother had

ever held me close like that to feed me. I sort of hoped she had done so. But right now, sitting on a log outside a shack somewhere in a place called Republic Flat, all I could handle was watching what I was seeing, Cora and her child.

Two wildflowers.

# CHAPTER
## 13

I NO LONGER HAD A TENT.

My earlier plan was to continue to ride south, but a typical Florida thunderstorm blew in, and I didn't feel like riding through it. Or having to sleep under only my slicker.

Cora said, "Sleep in the chicken shed."

If old Bad Murphy came home during the night, Cora explained, he'd get real upset to find me in the shack with her. So, along with several chickens, I bedded down in a shed that was open on one side and leaked on the other three. The roof could leak worse than Gusher after his Saturday night tanking of beer.

In the middle of the night, I was soaking wet and a mite chilly, so I decided I'd plead some indoor hospitality from Cora. As I was about to knock on the shack door, I spotted her shotgun where she'd left it after I'd dismounted, hours ago. A curious inspection of the shotgun, as I broke it open, showed me that the antique weapon was empty. Nobody home in the shell chamber. The barrel was bent and the homemade stock was held in place by rusting fence wire. Even if loaded it wasn't much of a weapon.

I knocked.

"Is that you, Bad Murphy?" I heard her ask.

"No, it's Bad Bodeen. I'm soaked clear to bone, and cold. Would you please permit me to come inside and dry out before I catch myself a case of the vapors? I won't trespass you, I promise."

The door opened a crack.

"Hush, the baby's sleeping."

"Sorry." I shivered.

"All right, in with you. But no funny stuff, hear?"

"I hear." Although smoky, it was cozy-warm inside, and it smelled of cooking and baby and Cora Emily Blike. Compared to the chicken shed, quite fragrant. Before closing the door, I brought in the sorrowful shotgun, handing it to Cora. "Take careful," I told her, "because it could go off and kill somebody." As I said it, I smiled, shooting her a knowing wink.

Cora sighed. "It ain't loaded."

"I know. And my guess is there isn't anybody named Bad Murphy. You maybe claim there is to scare people off."

She nodded slowly, looking downcast, and still wearing her raggy old dress that said Gold Medal Flour on it.

"Hey," I said, moving closer to the small cookstove, "if you want, I could be your Bad Bodeen."

Waiting, I had a hanker to be. Not once in my entire life had I ever had me a sweetheart, and I liked Cora more than Sue Louise. Also I had an itch to tell Cora the straight of it, so I did. Blurted it out. "I don't have a sweetheart. Leastwise, not right now."

She smiled softly. "Well, if you ask me, a handsome buck like you doggone ought." The feeble light from the stove painted her face a soft pretty amber. Unable to think of how I could express my sudden joy, I merely trembled. Cora noticed. "Snake out of those wet duds."

"Here?"

"You got to dry. Or else you'll maybe shimmy yourself into a fever." She approached me. "You don't have to be shy around me. I got raised among three brothers. If you've seen one bare backside, you seen 'em all."

Slipping out of my shirt, I couldn't help noticing how much Cora reminded me of my brother Tate. Both of them looked you square on and spoke what was thought.

"I'm fifteen," I said, even though I was coming up close to sixteen. "How old are you?"

Cora shrugged. "Not *that* old. But out here alone, I somedays feel ancient, doggone near twenty. And I'm starting to wonder how long I can support myself here, and my baby. It's tough to live on pride instead of beans."

She sure had a shiny way to say things.

I pulled off my boots. Cora helped. She also lent a yank with my jeans and socks. So there I sat on a crate beside the stove, wearing only my union suit. It was the short summer variety, and not a long john.

"Oh, skin it off, Bad Bodeen," she said as she turned her back to me. "I won't peek and spoil your virtue." I took it off, hung it up on a rafter peg, and looked around the shack for a corner to hide in. Cora tossed me a blanket. "You won't find no bedbugs in *my* quilts," she said, hands defiantly on her hips. "Early today I spread it over a hill of fire ants, and they ate every tick on it."

I grinned.

My mind was comparing Cora Blike to Sue Louise Hartberry, and a conclusion was reached real rapid. Sue Louise was like owning a photograph of a beautiful horse, but Cora was like my actual riding it. Cora was real as dirt. In a way, being so bright and all, she was sort of a young Mrs. Skagg.

It was a constant amazement to discover, one by each, all the things Cora Blike could do, and the store of problems she could handle. Using the blanket, Cora rubbed my cold body until I was warming up close to raw. It felt wonderful. Perhaps partly due to the fact that she was doing it.

"Right about now," Cora said, vigorously drying my hair with a corner of the blanket, "you're probable wondering who is Burlin's pa. Well, my family asked me too. I didn't tell them and I won't tattle to you neither. It's a personal part of my history. The Lord doesn't bake perfect people like cookies on a sheet. All of us got faults. Burlin ain't a fault, though." She smiled in the half-light. "He's a blessing."

"You live here alone?"

She nodded. "Back when my time came, I sought out a midwife, bore my baby, and then cleared away from home and family. More'n once I got itched to crawl back." She looked at me and stopped rubbing. "You thawing back to normal yet?"

"Yes, and thanks for the rub."

"You're welcome. Now come sleep beside me. But no romantic business. One baby is about all I can fend for right now. In a few years, or as soon as my boy grows up enough to help me, I just might pop another. I like babies. Always have, because if'n they hunger for something, they'll let you know straight away."

Cora led me to the bunk.

Even though I wasn't cold or wet anymore, my body had the shakes. But I was tired. So was Cora. Sometime in the night, Burlin fussed, and I was barely awake enough to realize that Cora got up and suckled him quiet, then returned to bed. My eyes closed, and before I knew it, the black of night had softened to a more friendly gray. Early sunlight stole into the shack between the board cracks. Outside, a rooster crowed, breaking open the morning like it was a fresh egg.

Waking up, I sudden looked deep into Cora Blike's blue eyes. "Hey," I asked, "are you ripe for breakfast?"

"Hey yourself. Get up," she whispered to me, "and poke the stove awake, empty its ashes, add wood, and perform it all silent, or else you'll wake up Burlin."

"I can't get up," I told her, "on account I'm jaybird-naked."

My clothes were still hanging on the peg where I had placed them to dry last evening. Cora said a salty word. Then she promised not to peek, so I got up and dressed myself in slightly damp clothes, tended the stove, and then went outside to hustle up some well water. We ate. I supplied my last corn dodger, coffee, plums, and a mixture of beans boiled with grits.

"Say," I said, "I don't guess you ever heard of a gentleman by the name of Mr. Dodge Yardell?"

Cora smiled. "Sure enough have. He's a fine old gentleman. Truth be, he stops along here every so while, and brings me an alive chicken, or possum meat." She paused. "How come you know him?"

"I don't." After loading a fork of grits into my mouth, I munched, swallowed, and then told Cora Blike that Mr. Yardell was a long-ago friend of my father's. She seemed a mite surprised to learn about that, but then said that I must have a good daddy.

"He's been like a grandpa to me, Laddy. He knows I'm only a squatter in this old shack. Even though I'm a nobody, he's nice."

"You're not a nobody. You're Burlin's ma. But even if you weren't you'd be my friend," I said. "By the way, do you happen to know exactly where Mr. Yardell lives?"

Cora pointed with a spoon. "South of here. But don't poke me how far, because it'd only be a guess if'n I answer. S'pose if you ride your horse south you might stumble into where he lives. Or maybe not." Cora smiled again. "Gee, it's oddy you are actual looking to meet Dodge. Life does twist and curl worse'n a bottomland brook."

"Guess it does."

"Well, I hope you locate him. I looked for his place one time, but never did find it. How come you're looking up Dodge?"

I didn't answer Cora right away, because I was weighing whether I should or shouldn't. Mrs. Skagg once remarked that you can't trust everybody. But then she said that trusting nobody was equal as empty. Her solution was to have a few real close friends and trust the living heck of them, and do it forever.

"Cat got your tongue?" Cora asked me.

I grinned, because the feeling that I was about to trust a stranger who'd taken me in, so to speak, was a right pleasant thought. "Well," I said, "I'm fixing to hunt me some wild horses. And it so happens that Mr. Dodge Yardell is some sort of an expert. I'm hoping he'll lend me a hand."

"Shucks," said Cora, "if an extra hand is all you're looking for, I'd be glad to tag along."

Her answer surprised me. "You would?"

"Honest would. You're about the only decent boy company I've seen around here for a long time. Don't think I'm intending to let *you* get away without a bruise and scratches."

Cora smiled, and my world smiled too.

*She likes me!*

"The trouble is," Cora said, "it might be dangerous for Burlin, because wild horses are a lot bigger than a baby." I looked at Burlin Blike. He sure was a tyke, rather small, and I couldn't think of an answer for Cora. As the enthusiasm for horse hunting was melting off her face, sobering her, I knew right then that she wasn't going to come along. "Besides," she said, "I don't have a horse."

"Evelyn," I sighed.

"Who?"

"My mule, the one that got killed by that swamp gator. If I only had Evelyn, you could ride her."

It was Cora's turn to sigh. "I don't guess I'll be coming along with you and Dodge. But don't sadden yourself over it. Just be certain you stop by here on your way north, going home to Kickaloo. You hear me, Bad Bodeen?"

I grinned. "I honest will."

"Good. I like you, Laddy. So you can ride yourself south, but not without remembering me and Burlin. I'm going to harbor you. Some people got a heart colder than outdoor molasses. Not you. You're warming to look at, and to eat with." Cora took a deep breath. "Now," she said, "I reckon you ought to hitch up your belt, spit on your hands, and kiss me a so-long."

"Kiss you?"

Cora tightened her fists. "I ain't poison."

I kissed her. And she sure wasn't.

# CHAPTER
## 14

I RODE SOUTH.

Inside, my heart was clog dancing, and I was feeling happier than a sweaty horse rolling in loose dirt.

"Cora," I said. "Cora, Cora, Cora."

Well, I'd final shed my timidity amongst young ladies, and I had Miss Cora Emily Blike to thank. Wow! I'd actual slept all night near a *girl*. So it had been a girl and a baby and no trespassing, but Cora certain was a girl and a half. I'd best remember some of the things she told me, the way to get ticks or bedbugs out of a blanket . . . stretch it over an anthill, and allow the ants to pick it clean. And how trouble comes in two sizes, quick and slow. Or about pride and beans.

"Brownie," I told my bay mare, "Cora is easy as smart as she is pretty."

Pretty as a song.

Early this morning I'd kissed her, *me,* Laddy Bodeen of the Buckle Tee ranch. I had actual *done* it. As I rode the mare south, I kept licking my lips, trying to retaste Cora Blike, my favorite flavor. To heck with vanilla and chocolate, throwing in raspberry and cherry and orange, lemon, and lime.

"Mrs. Skagg," I said aloud, "I'm having one heck of an exciting enterprise, more than I'd ever bargained for. Wow."

It made me think of back home, of chores, of all my summer
duties on the Buckle Tee, such as pinching up dirt out of post
holes to line in a new fence. Not much of it would ever be quite
straight enough to please Tate. He wanted our fences straighter
than a fresh-tuned banjo string.

Helping my brother wasn't fun. One time, we were working
on a stud horse, and all I had to do was heft up a hind hoof and
also hoist its tail, while Tate took a look at the stud's front leg.
But then the hornets came. One stung me. As I dropped the rear
hoof, the stud whipped his head around and sank his teeth into
the meat of Tate's shoulder.

I could still hear Tate's holler.

Blood soaked his shirt. And the pain about twisted his sanity
into madness.

Afterward, when Mrs. Skagg's needle and thread were effort-
ing to stitch my brother back into one piece, to close the gaping
wound, Mrs. Skagg had asked him how badly the stallion's bite
had hurt him.

Tate said, "It holds your interest."

True enough, he was Sam Bodeen reborn.

From that time forward, I had always wondered if Tate had
any feelings at all. Gusher claimed no. Slim was usual quiet on
the matter as he'd cotton to keep his job. That left Mrs. Skagg.
She adored him. Perhaps she could see virtues in Tate that the rest
of us oversaw, not because virtue wasn't there. It was because
Tate's hickory nature refused to allow any lyric to lighten his
load.

Tate was pettish.

That was merely his way, and to know my brother was to
accept him, as is. Buy the whole package or leave it fallow in

the field. Me, I bought the package. He was family. And if anyone ever crossed Tate, he'd have Laddy Bodeen to look him in the eye and say . . . "Back off, you're talking to *my brother.*"

Brownie nickered.

Snapping myself alert, I saw a very welcome sight. Another water tower. That meant that Brownie and I were progressing closer to where, according to my map, Dodge Yardell lived.

My mind was still digging fence-post holes, and then filling them with cedar posts that had been, according to Tate's instruction, soaked in creosote, an oily antiseptic liquid used to pickle the wood. That's how Tate Bodeen ordered our fences, and that's how they stood. Nobody at the Buckle Tee would dare stand up against how my brother wanted it done, and this was exactly why Tate Bodeen was going to become one successful rancher. He knew what had to be and ordered it so. No variation. Some of our neighbors insisted that scrub-oak or pine fence was a lot cheaper, without bothering to mess with the creosote, but Tate wouldn't agree. Tate's line of thinking was correct as his boundaries.

I rode into a village.

To be truthful straight, I almost rode right beyond before I could say "whoa." The name of the place, one citizen informed me, was Confederation, Florida. It sure was a blink-and-miss-it town, and a chewer could spit twice and drown the place. A sign in a window said RESTAURANT, and then, underneath, there was a promise in small print that read "stove chow." I stopped and had some.

Between swallows, I asked the restaurant's only other patron if he'd ever heard of Mr. Dodge Yardell. "Due south," the man said. "You can't miss it." I thanked him.

Confederation didn't take long to ride through. I could have held my breath and made it all the way.

In less than a quarter of a mile, riding south, I could swear that there had been no town, no Confederation, and nary another human soul to argue with. Nothing but open Florida flatland, and I was starting to understand why somebody, smarter than the rest, had decided to name this territory Republic Flat.

The sun climbed higher, hotter, and the smell of my shirt reminded me that soon I'd be needing what Gusher Plant called a once-a-skunk bath. My shirt certain begged for a hard soaping.

Checking my compass, I knew that the bay mare and I were heading due south, and sooner or later something had to happen. Republic Flat was flat for real. Griddle flat and griddle hot. My shirt was sweaty-wet, so I stopped beneath a palm grove to cool Brownie and myself. I pulled off her saddle and bridle in order to allow her to graze. As for me, I took off my soaking shirt.

It was difficult to think about anything or anyone except Cora Blike, who tasted sweeter than gooseberry preserve. She seemed sort of like food, or something cooling to drink on a hot dry evening. Thoughts of Cora were bathing me clean.

Moving on, the mare and I came to a crick that was plump from fresh rain, the storm of last night. The horse drank and so did I. The water tasted clear and delicious. Like wine. My mind kept wondering what everyone back at the Buckle Tee was doing about now. I could hear Tate, see Gusher, smell Mrs. Skagg's baking. And inhale a whiff of her too.

"Brownie," I said, "we got to push, so you'll have to wear the saddle." After the blanket, the leather seemed so heavy and cumbersome, but at least I'd be light for her to carry. All I weighed was 130 pounds.

I neck-reined her south and we were off again.

Perhaps my greatest hunk of luck on the trip, I was thinking, was in my selection of this bay mare. She sure was proving to be one dandy of a horse, never seeming to grow tired, ears always up and alert and forward, and her late-afternoon gait trotted along as brightly as a first-dance fiddle.

Ahead, up in the air I saw a trio of buzzards slowly floating around and around, drawing black circles against a white searing sky. One buzzard dropped, then another, and as I rode, I discovered what had captivated their attention and whetted their hunger.

A dead horse.

Riding closer, I could see that it was a stallion. A gray dapple. As I approached, the three buzzards flapped about thirty or forty feet distant, screeching and scolding, annoyed that my arrival had held up their rotting meal.

As I rode around the dead stallion, I noticed his hoofs. *No iron.* Could the stallion be wild? No brand on the flank that showed, but that didn't necessarily mean a brand wasn't kissing dirt on the bottom side. Dismounting, I pushed up the two hind legs and, with some effort, managed to roll the horse over. No brand. And no shoes on its hoofs. This could mean only one thing.

The stallion had been wild.

It also told me about the horse's death. My guess was that this stallion had challenged the stud of the wild band. They had fought. Here lay the loser. His neck and chest were torn by teeth marks, and also by some bloody bruises where a front hoof had struck. The skull also appeared to be partly crushed. Between the teeth of the dead stallion were several tufts of white horse hair. Very white. The teeth were in good condition. This horse wasn't old.

"Young stud," I said to the dead animal, "you sure did challenge a helping of white trouble."

We moved away from the smell.

After about another ten miles, I happened to spot a clearing off to my right. There was a distant ranch, a small one, yet there was something very calm and disciplined about the place, even from so far away. Brownie trumpeted her nose, making that unique flutter of a sound that only a horse can do. Another horse answered, from nearby. Riding in, I saw a beauty of a palomino mare walking our way, as though she wanted to greet us proper. On her flank was a burn. Curiously I neck-reined my bay to a position where I could read the brand.

It was D-bar-Y.

I smiled.

"Brownie," I said to my mare, "I'd take a guess that we made it."

My body was feeling more than a mite stiff from an all-day ride, plus the fact that three days ago a rodeo bull had loaded me up with misery. So I kicked out of the saddle. Then I hobbled Brownie, pulled off her bridle to comfort her mouth, sat down in the shade of a live-oak tree, leaned against the tree, and closed my eyes.

I wasn't honest intending to sleep.

It just caught me from behind.

A real sweet dream about Cora Blike would have suited me right about fine, but no such fortune. Instead, I was back behind an arena chute at the Kickaloo Junior Rodeo, about to fork myself astride a bull. I could sort of hear the band. But the bull didn't quite seem to be a bull any longer. It wasn't even bovine. I was on the back of an alligator, and I could hear Evelyn braying her hee-haw, sawing the sound into me like I was a hunk of stubborn wood. I wanted to wake up, but my horror of a dream wouldn't quit. It kept grinding. Against my spine, I could feel the hard trunk of the oak tree pressing against me, and it wasn't too comforting. Also my neck was drooping to one side, and hurting me some. My clothes seemed to be drenched in sweat and felt damp and clammy.

"Mrs. Skagg," I wanted to say.

Somewhere I could hear my brother's voice. Tate was giving me advice on how to ride a gator in a rodeo. Cora and Burlin were watching me, knowing that I wouldn't be able to stay aboard the alligator for eight seconds.

"Chute number two," I thought I heard the rodeo's bullhorn announce. "Bill Tarky . . . and Sue Louise Hartberry . . . coming out of chute number two . . . on . . . a motorcycle."

"Cora," said Bill Tarky. "I'll take Cora."

"No," I said. "You dang won't."

"Wake up," somebody told me. The voice I was now hearing didn't belong to a loudspeaker or to a rodeo. In fact, it was a new voice, one that I'd never before listened up. Then I heard a very sharp sound and it was close to my left ear.

*Click!*

Opening my eyes, I felt the steely hardness on my neck, right below my ear. Then I realized what the *click* was.

A gun hammer.

# CHAPTER
## 15

MY HEAD TURNED.

The man's weapon wasn't exactly pointed to add another nostril to my head, but only a few inches off. It was a Colt pistol. Then I saw a hand, a shirtsleeve, then a leathery face that needed a shave. With one hand, he held his revolver, but in the other he was holding my Buckle Tee branding iron.

"Now," he said in a surprisingly velvet voice, "let's do it all slow and easy." He paused. "On your feet."

I got up.

No longer was the hawgleg Colt pointed at me, yet my branding iron certain was, and hardly in a friendly manner. Holding his pistol toward the ground, yet ready, the man pushed the ⧉T business end of the iron under my chin.

"Stranger," he said, "I think you've got some explaining due me. You're on my land with a foreign branding iron, which sort of hints you might be tempted to alter my stock." His voice wasn't angry or even unpleasant. He sounded calm and intelligent, perhaps even reasonable. But then he gave my jaw a nudge with the brand. Not very gently. "And it'll come to you as a surprise, boy, but I happen to know where you borrowed that iron. You took it off a friend of mine. His name is Sam Bodeen."

He lowered the iron an inch or two. "Talk up," he said softly. "But if you tell me an untrue story, you might be locating yourself in harm's way."

I gulped.

"My name is Ladd Bodeen. Sam's my father."

As the gray eyes softened, they seemed to be studying my facial features . . . eyes, nose, mouth, and the shape of my head in general.

"Yes," he said at last, "you're Sam's boy."

Slowly I let out a breath that I'd been holding inside me for most of a minute. But I was still wondering who this man was, even though I was willing to take a stab at it.

"Sir, are you Mr. Dodge Yardell?"

The man nodded. Then he offered me a hand to shake and I took it.

So, seeing as he was sizing me up, I helped myself to a thorough look at him. He seemed to be about the same age as my father, between sixty and seventy, but of a slighter build. Papa once was thick, this man was almost bone-lean, but very resolute in his manner. There seemed to be a gentle strength in him. His mustache was a soft gray, almost white, and he was wearing at least a two-day growth of gray beard stubble. The shirt he wore was also gray but it once might have been a blue cotton workshirt. Yet the shirt had no collar and it exposed a bronzed and sunburnt neck. His trousers looked worn but clean, again a millworker blue that had been mostly soaped and boiled to colorless. On his sleeves he wore black arm garters. There was a tear in one pant leg, the frayed edges of which were being reunited by a silver safety pin. Over the shirt he wore a black and white cowhide vest. On his lower wrists, a pair of brown and blue bracelets, exactly alike. They looked to be coral and turquoise. His belt buckle was a generous silver oval with a *Y* in the center. Around his neck on a leather thong hung what appeared to be the tip of a deer antler, about two inches long.

His hands were gloved. There were leather roping cuffs on his forearms, to cinch a rope around. Tate wore a similar pair. His boots were old and worn, yet seemed to be well oiled and serviceable for years to come. A rowel-wheel spur trailed each boot.

He stared at me. "You want supper?"

The word sent hunger pangs through my stomach. "Oh, I sure would, Mr. Yardell. Please."

He nodded. "Come along then."

Nearby stood a small but sturdy Morgan mare, a chestnut. The man swung up into the saddle with a light and easy movement. He held the reins loosely in his left hand. Waiting, he wheeled the horse in a circle with only the slightest gesture. After I mounted my bay mare, the two of us rode beside one another. It was a pleasure to watch him sit a saddle, like he had become part of it, part of the Morgan too.

"What brings you this far south?" he asked me.

"Horses," I said.

"Ah, then that explains the branding iron. You're down this way to hunt horses."

I nodded. "I'm after the whole band."

"How come Sam didn't come?" As he asked the question, there seemed to be a hardness in his voice that was usual so soft.

I hauled in a breath. "He's been ill for a time. In his mind. Actual, for thirteen years, ever since Mama died."

He looked my way. "Lola May's gone?" As he asked the question there was genuine sorrow in his eyes.

"Yes, since I was two. I never really got to know her. And

not Papa either, on account he just sits and stares and hardly ever speaks a word."

Mr. Yardell shook his head. "Sad. I'm powerful sorry to learn about it."

I sensed he meant it.

Together we rode to his place. It was a tidy-looking ranch, orderly, as if things there knew that Mr. Dodge Yardell would not welcome disarray. I saw no litter. Even the chickens were inside an enclosure. So were three calves. Mr. Yardell dismounted, undid his cinch, and then, after pulling off his saddle, toted it to a tackroom. I did likewise. We turned out our mounts, his Morgan and my bay, into an open meadow. There were no fences in view.

Mr. Yardell was noticing my mare.

"Good animal," he said quietly.

"I learned that," I said.

He looked at me for a moment. "Yes, if you rode her this distant, I'd suspect you've weighed her worth." He paused. "And no doubt she's probable measured yours."

Charlie ate with us.

He was a friendly Seminole who lived at Mr. Yardell's place and worked for food and wages. His complete name, he told me, was Charlie No Water. He sure wasn't a champion of conversation. If'n he talked it was mostly to God.

Mr. Yardell explained that, a good number of years ago, he had found Charlie beaten up and close to dead. He had also been about to die from thirst, so he'd pointed at his throat and said, "Charlie No Water."

His Seminole name was Chalo, but the Charlie seemed to suit him better.

Supper consisted of beef chunks, onions, peppers, carrots, all fried in a black skillet and dumped on boiled rice. Mr. Dodge

Yardell could have hired himself out as a cook for a king. His biscuits were lighter than morning and served in a round tin with plenty of sweet butter to melt inside each one. I ate about seven biscuits and was reaching for another.

"Go outside 'em," Mr. Yardell told me during the meal. "Charlie and I aren't growing anymore. You be. So sink 'em into you, Laddy. A mite of wheat flour'll widen you some."

As soon as supper was hidden, Charlie grabbed a cookpot and scrubbed it clean. So did Mr. Yardell, and I helped. We all pulled an oar. A combining of spirit and suds put away the pots, pans, and dishes. With those men, it didn't seem a mite like labor. Only fun. Mr. Dodge Yardell's place was a happy location to live at.

Charlie left. He exited without so much as an utterance. Sort of drifted up a chimney like smoke.

Dodge's shack contained one luxury, an item he called a dofunny.

A tiny piano.

As it turned out, Mr. Yardell could only play one song, "Genevieve, My Genevieve." Sitting down at the piano, he actual played the ballad, and also sang it in a more than pleasasnt voice. "Oh Genevieve, sweet Genevieve. The days may come. The days may go . . ."

It was entertaining.

When the song final wore itself out and quit, Mr. Yardell again admitted that "Genevieve" was the only song he could hammer all the way through on the keyboard. Yet he performed it passable, so well that I had me a hankering to master the words so I could sing it along beside him. Like a duet. As he sang, I sort of became homesick to hear Gusher Plant play the harmonica and to hear Slim Service's singing.

Slim, as I recalled, would sometimes get up in the middle of the night, during a thunderboomer, and warble a melody to our beefs. Just to stay 'em still. He'd do this in rain. Tate told me all about it one time. And then he said that he'd rather go busted fall-down shirttail broke than fire Mrs. Skagg or Slim or old Gusher Plant. Hearing him say such tapped me on the shoulder as if to say what a decent boss Tate Bodeen was, and forever would be. He really didn't manage only a ranch.

Tate had somehow stirred all of us into a family cookie batter, but what we poured ourselves into would be up to each one of us.

"Do you sing?" Mr. Yardell asked me.

"No," I said. "I'm what Slim calls a natural-born crow." I then explained. "Slim Service is a hand on our ranch, the Buckle Tee."

Mr. Yardell nodded. "Son, I'm aware of your brand. Have been for a passel of years." He paused to shake his head. "In the future, Laddy, try not to ride into another man's territory with a strange branding iron. It happens to be a real rapid way to get hanged."

As he spoke, Mr. Yardell was still seated at his little piano, looking up at my face, telling me things that I sudden realized I'd best remember. To own up honest, I'd maybe been a simpleton to tote a branding iron to someone else's grazing land, and perhaps I had been fortunate not to have wound up shot.

Or hanged.

My throat tightened.

"Tell me about Sam," Mr. Yardell said. "I always wanted to visit, but I had me a reason not to."

"Mostly," I reported, "he only sits and stares straight ahead. But when I told him that Tate—he's my older brother—and I were fixing to ride south and try to throw a rope on a mustang, Papa's face lit up. Not much. Yet he seemed to be aware of our plan."

"Your brother didn't come along."

"No. Instead he got himself kicked by a hoof because of a rattlesnake. So I came lonesome." I grinned. "It's my first enterprise."

Getting up slowly from the piano stool, Mr. Yardell stretched his arms, then relaxed. "Maybe," he said, "I can final say I'd like to see Sam Bodeen. And if there's a way to help you and your brother bring Sam back his senses, I be pleased to do my bit. Right now, guess I'll dent my pillow."

"Thanks for supper," I said, "and for the use of your spare room. Tomorrow, I'd like to hunt horses."

Mr. Yardell held up a restraining hand. "Tomorrow," he said, "I got a horse to gentle. Stick around, and I'll show you how enjoyable it is."

I smiled. "I sure will."

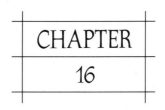

# CHAPTER

# 16

I SLEPT LATE.

At the D-bar-Y, there was no Tate and Mrs. Skagg to warn me that five o'clock had best not catch me napping. So I slept until almost six-thirty. This, on Tate's clock, was doggone near to noon.

In the kitchen, Mr. Yardell was perking a pot of coffee. Seeing me, he said nothing, but cracked six eggs into a skillet that was already wet with bacon grease. We both ate, saying little. I was used to quiet. Tate Bodeen wouldn't say *mud* if he'd spooned himself a mouthful.

"This morning," I asked Mr. Yardell, "according to what you said last night, you intend to break a horse?"

He sighed. "*Break* isn't my word." He took a gulp of black coffee. "If you were a horse, or a teapot, would you like somebody *breaking* you?"

"Don't guess so," I said.

"Me either. Far as I'm concerned, horses make better friends than a lot of people do. And I'll trust a horse. Right from the start, if you *gentle* a horse, befriending him, he'll add a deal of sunshine to your life. He'll ease your working; then on Sunday, a horse will do you ample proud if you hanker to show off. Or show him off to your neighbors."

I didn't quite know how to ask the one important question. That being, would Mr. Dodge Yardell team up with me and help me round up the wild band? Not knowing, and a mite apprehensive to ask, I held quiet. After breakfast, the two of us went outdoors to the cordon, where a young brown colt, full grown, looked at us as though we'd just arrived from Saturn.

"Never been rode," Dodge said. "What's worse, his owner claims he can't be."

"And you're about to top him?"

The man shook his head. "Not me. No sense to scare the poor animal to death or bust his spirit." He pulled an orange vegetable from his pocket. "Boy, oft times a carrot can teach a better lesson than a quirt."

In my mind, I could envision my brother. I had seen a quirt dangling from Tate's wrist whenever he broke horses. A thong loop held it to his wrist, then a short handle, and below, a set of long rawhide lashes. According to my brother, a quirt could earn the respect of a horse with only a few licks.

No quirt hung from Mr. Dodge Yardell.

Only a carrot.

"Laddy," he said in his velvety voice, "what we have here is a green colt. He's young. Sort of like you. Doesn't yet know what this old world is all about, or how it'll treat him. Rich, or raw. If it's raw, then he won't turn out to be much better than ornery rodeo stock. But if it's rich, this young colt will begin to realize that maybe life is pleasant, and that a two-legged friend means a carrot instead of a spur."

He snapped the carrot into short bits, handing all of them to me.

"Here," he said, "let this animal know that you've come in

friendship. My guess is, knowing who owns the critter, that this young horse has never in his whole life tasted a carrot. So let him savor it."

Holding a small section of the carrot in the flat of my hand, I allowed the colt to inhale its flavor. He grunted softly, then lowered his head, as I felt those soft searching lips nibbling, seizing, then I heard the munching of strong young teeth tasting a treat.

"To train an animal," Mr. Yardell said, "it's so much quicker and easier to guide a brain instead of a body. Work on pleasure, not pain. Show him that life is worth celebrating. And it really doesn't take that much. A carrot. And a stroking. Teach this youngster that living is something to enjoy, not to endure."

His voice was tranquil, near to churchy. It was steady, contained, as though it gave him unmeasured pleasure to make a new friend out of a green horse.

As I watched his leathery hands move on the colt's neck, I thought about Crankshaft. I remembered the cutting strap, an electric prodder, the noise and the stink of smoking, drinking, cussing humanity that could have offended an animal that only wanted a meadow, a sip of cool water, and grass.

He looked at me.

"Boy, do you know why Mr. Edgerton had to van this colt all the way over here, and bestow him to my custody?"

"No," I admitted.

"It's because Billy Jack Edgerton tells me that he's been having more'n a wisp of trouble with this young animal. As he informed me about it, I was thinking . . . I'll bet this here green colt is having trouble with y'all. When he got here, his attitude was all fear. Ears always back. Eyes widened. If you wanted this horse to sweat, all you had to do was enter the cordon. He wouldn't tolerate a human in his corral. Shy away. And his hide would sweat. It was fear. I could taste it in his whinny."

Leaving me for a minute, Mr. Yardell disappeared into his barn, then returned carrying what appeared to be a colorful Mexican shawl. The colors were slightly faded.

"What's that?"

"Oh, this is called a *rebozo*. It's a mite lighter than a saddle blanket. Years ago, I had me a Mexican lady for a housekeeper. Mrs. Sanchez, her name was. White hair. Older than sin. Had a way with her though, especially around horses, and her trick was this here *rebozo*. She'd rub it along the spine of the most ornery bucker of a bronc you could ever dread to witness, and he'd comply to it. Stroke by stroke, he'd gentle."

As I fed more carrot to the colt, Mr. Yardell used the *rebozo* to caress the horse's flank. He responded. At first with nerves; then slowly, with an obvious enjoyment, because the shawl was offering pleasure. A rubdown.

"He likes it," I said.

Mr. Yardell nodded. "Even a human takes pleasure in a back rub. I had me a friend, Short Callum, who'd got gored by a bull. He had to go to a hospital for some cutting and sewing. Afterward, he said the one experience he treasured most was a hospital nurse rubbing his back. She used a special alcohol. Short said it felt so righteous comforting, it was better than drinking it."

"Do people bring their horses to you for fixing?"

Mr. Yardell grinned. "Indeed so. But the trouble is, they usual leave the wrong critter. It's people who need repair and correcting, not horses. Yes, it's the human beings who most ought to be straightened on a fresh track. You know who should be trotting around inside this cordon? I'll tell you who. Ought to be Mr. Billy Jack Edgerton himself, and not this horse."

I watched his hands working.

Slowly, with a gentle patience, he guided the *rebozo* along the colt's body, all over, sometimes pausing to let the affection soak into one particular area, as though trying to heal a wound.

He smiled.

"This," he said quietly, "is what I should be doing for Billy Jack, the gentleman who owns this fearing animal. You and I ought to cart ourselves over to his place and snug him all over with a *rebozo,* to settle him like a mare beyond season." Easily, he guided the young colt's head around to where his hand met his animal's upper neck. "Here," he said, "between a horse's ears, there's what I call a spirit bump, a little mound, like the rising pelvis of a loving woman." He took my hand. "Here, right here, feel it with your fingers. That's where it's lying. And you'll reach a horse so easy by touching it."

I felt it.

Mr. Yardell was right.

Between the horse's ears was a slight rise, not a bone, but it was harder than flesh yet softer than shank.

"Feel it?" he asked me.

I nodded.

"Well, I don't honest know," said Dodge, "what it's rightfully called, but I label it a spirit bump. Let's just say it's a lump of intelligence. Trouble is, most humans can't admit that an animal has any brains. Not true. If you work with an animal's mind, you'll have a success with the remainder of him. Only way to train a horse is to make the wrong thing difficult and the right thing pleasant."

It took two hours of work with the *rebozo* to settle the colt enough to permit a saddle blanket across his backbone. At last, he allowed it. Later, a saddle. All the while, Mr. Yardell talked to the colt as though the animal was a person. A friend. He even asked the colt if the saddle was maybe a pound or two too cumbersome.

"Now," he said, "is that a burden? If it is, we'll just remove it and let you stroll around the corral for a spell. But, sooner or later, you'll have to carry some weight. You're strong. You'll be able. That's right, strong as a horse."

Mr. Yardell laughed.

So did I.

"Along about late afternoon," Mr. Yardell told me, "this animal might be ready to receive a snaffle bit."

When he final tried it, the colt struck with a front hoof, a movement that almost flashed with its quickness.

"Easy," Mr. Yardell told the animal. "I know you have spunk inside you, and that's normal. You can let it out some around here. That's what it's all about, our place. You're boarding at the D-bar-Y now. So you're permitted a spark or two. It's part of being young and alive." He turned to me. "Never be afraid of becoming too lenient with a horse. It certain beats being too hard-handed."

It turned out to be a long day.

"You're lighter than I am," he told me. "So it'll be your honor to swing a leg up into his saddle. If he bucks you off, into riddance, we'll just do the next best thing, and that's try it tomorrow."

I vaulted up, very slowly.

The colt's body turned rigid. Yet he didn't buck. He accepted my weight, as if to admit that he could welcome the closeness of another body next to him.

I talked to the horse. "Good boy." Reaching my hand forward I patted his neck, creating a sound, a feeling that he could hear as well as feel.

My bootheels touched him lightly. He responded by trotting

a tight circle inside the cordon, causing no trouble, his head held up high and his ears forward as though anticipating life. Mr. Yardell smiled, and then used the same words to me as I had said to the colt.

"Good boy."

# CHAPTER
## 17

WE ATE SUPPER.

Not wanting to become a burden, I told Mr. Yardell that I could contribute some food to his pantry, and I offered him what little I had left. It was potatoes, white beans, and dried plums. He refused.

"Golly no," he told me. "You're a guest here, Laddy, and you're Sam's spawn. Besides, you helped earn a keep today with that green colt. And you kept both of us company. You'll be welcome here as long as you tarry."

"Thanks," I said.

We sat outside on a pair of old chairs, watching the sun slowly retreat like it was weary from making Florida grow.

I told him about Cora. The whole story.

"You spent a night with her?" he asked me. Then his face frowned. "I hope you didn't deposit a baby inside her. She's hiking through life uphill."

Quickly I explained that we'd sort of slept apart like a brother and sister, but Mr. Yardell still gave me a cold questioning glance.

"Honest," I said. "I don't trespass on girls."

He grinned. "I believe you."

"It's the straight-out truth," I said, "and it won't change, sir, whether you believe me or you don't."

"Fair enough."

The two of us sat silent for a spell.

"Gusher Plant told me a few things about you, and about Short Callum."

Mr. Yardell shook his head. "All lies."

Laughing, I said, "Gusher sometimes can rubber a fact or two. My brother, Tate, claims that Gush can take a deep breath and inflate the truth like a balloon." I paused. "But he also told me, sir, that you can woodcarve."

The man nodded. "That I do enjoy." He stood up. "How would you like to come see my workshop?"

"I sure would."

"Let's go."

We walked to one of the buildings near his barn. Taking a key from his pocket, Mr. Yardell unlocked the padlock and opened the large double doors.

I looked inside. Walking in, it was like entering Paradise. Even though I was fifteen years old, I suddenly felt half my age, or less. Everywhere I looked, I saw small wooden horses, some painted, others still the natural color of raw wood. No two horses were alike.

"As you can see," Mr. Yardell said, "I carve my animals in different poses." He touched a pink pony with his hand. "This one is a stander. Every hoof except one is flat on the ground. Now this one"—he pointed to a yellow horse with its front hoofs raised up—"is what they call a prancer." Indicating a light blue pony, he said, "With all four hoofs up, you have a jumper."

I didn't know where to look first. It was a candy store of small horses, each prettier than the others.

Not once in my whole life had I ever had myself a ride on

a merry-go-round, or even seen one. A picture of one in a magazine, but that's as close to a merry-go-round as I'd made it. Kids who had ridden a merry-go-round years ago at carnivals and fairs kept talking about the experience close to all summer.

"I never rode a merry-go-round," I said, the words pouring out of me without much previous thought. More of a wish than an admission. "Not even once."

Dodge Yardell gestured with an invitational sweep of an arm and hand. "In that case, seeing as you're not fixing to grow any younger, or smaller, pretend yourself to a ride." He began a grin. "Don't worry. I won't tell on you."

"It's okay?"

"Yes. Climb aboard."

Being very careful, I mounted each completed pony, the pink, the yellow, blue, red, white . . . until I'd sat on the hard wooden saddles of all of them. Every stander, prancer, and jumper.

Mr. Yardell was smiling. "By gosh, you're the first kid I ever seen riding my horses. It's a first time for me too. And I'm thankful you're Sam Bodeen's boy."

On the wall of the workshop a wooden sign was hanging. Not a large one. The sign was not much more than a foot square, but had a fancy design. I read what it said:

PHILADELPHIA

TOBOGGAN

COMPANY

"What's the middle word mean?" I asked.

"Oh, it's some sort of a snow sled with a curled-up nose. I don't guess the contraption has much to do with a merry-go-round. But seeing as you asked me, that's the name of the company I carve my ponies for. Every couple-three years, they'll write me a letter to find out how many wooden jobs I've finished and painted, then they'll send a truck here and pay cash on delivery."

"Are you the only person who can carve merry-go-round ponies like this?"

"No. There's a Mr. D. C. Muller that's real good at it, so they say. And a fellow whose name is Parker, but I don't guess I know his first name. Also there's a pair of brothers, Gustav and William Dentzel. Plenty of others. It doesn't take a whole lot of artistry. Just patience."

Looking at one of the painted ponies, I noticed that the pony's right side was quite fancy compared to his left. For one thing, the curls of his mane fell on the right side of his neck, and the saddle was also set with jewels on that side. The left flank, again, was plain. So I asked Mr. Yardell about it, seeing as all of his ponies were that way, fancy on the right. Before answering, he drew a circle in the dirt floor, using an old hoe handle.

"To begin with," he said, "in America, a merry-go-round always turns counterclockwise. A carnival crowd only sees a horse's right flank, known as the romance side, designed to be gussy for the onlookers. The inside of the horse is never really seen, so it can be plainer than raw grits."

My careful examination of all of his horses prompted more questions which Mr. Yardell didn't seem to mind answering.

"How come there's this big hole in the prancers and jumpers, but not on the standers?"

"Because the standers stand on the outside, while the two inside rings work up and down on a pole to which a child can cling. There's a reason for it. The standers don't rise and fall with the music, so there's no axle pole in those."

Each hoof was painted silver on the bottom, as if the ponies had been shod. Manes and tails were curving and graceful. Although carved out of wood, they appeared to be soft and flowing and recently currycombed.

"How do you do it?" I asked. "It sure as certain's got to be difficult work."

"Not that difficult. All you do is eliminate the wood you don't want, and then whatever's left over is a horse."

At his workbench, I inspected his tools. Most of them hung against the wall, their necks pinched by pairs of pegs, all in neat tidy rows, points down, like brown-helmeted soldiers. A silent army of one-legged warriors.

I selected a tool.

"What's this?"

"An awl. It's used for punching a small hole into which I can add a shiny stud on a saddle. Here. These rows of studs all began with one hole beside another. Children are like crows and jay-birds. They like objects that shine. Kids shine too."

Looking at the horses, I could nearly hear the music of a merry-go-round, and the entire workshop seemed to spin in one rainbow of a circle. I felt so proud that Mr. Dodge Yardell was a friend of my father, Mr. Sam Bodeen of the Buckle Tee cattle outfit.

"Mr. Yardell," I said slowly, "I certain would like to invite you to visit Tate and me, at our ranch. It would allow you to see Papa, your friend."

He didn't answer at once, because he had selected a tool and was gouging out a ridge in the mane of an unpainted pony. Then he looked my way.

"Maybe," he said. "Thanks for the invite."

I hung on to my bowels. "However," I said, "before that, I was sort of wondering if you would help me hunt up horses. We could be horse hunters together."

He stared at me silently.

"Mustangs," I said. "We could split the profits fifty-fifty. Half and half."

He smiled. "I know what fifty-fifty means."

"Sorry," I said. "Total it up to enthusiasm instead of mean manners. All I wanted to say is, let's go round up that band of wild horses, the way you and Papa used to, back in the old days."

Before answering, his hands were stroking a raw wooden pony, touching its flanks, rubbing what almost seemed to be the velvet of its nose. He touched the pony as though it were alive.

"Freedom," he said.

"I don't understand."

"There's something so majestic about an animal or a human who has made the discovery of being free. It's so rare. Sometimes, I think I'm the only free man alive. Yet I dang found it. And it means so much to me that I don't guess I could work up the gumption to deny it to any other living critter, man or beast."

As he spoke, the tendons across my belly began to tighten, as though I was afraid of what his eventual answer might tell me. And it made me wonder how I'd ever begin to capture a band of mustangs, all alone, even if I found them. It seemed impossible.

For some reason, I asked Mr. Yardell about what he meant by freedom, because it somehow seemed to be more important than being a horse hunter.

"Freedom," he said, "is doing what you doggone well please, bowing to no man, yet respecting all living creatures. It's standing tall, without becoming taller by stepping on somebody. Or stomping on him. There's a song to it. Maybe a poem. No man could ever explain to another man about freedom, because it has to be lived. Perhaps it's knowing that no kingdom or government can order you about. Freedom is standing your ground with a polite defiance. It is realizing that you are independent enough to say *I think* instead of *we think*. It's being alone and liking it."

I hauled in a breath. "In other words, sir, you're saying that you won't enter into a partnership with me to hunt horses?" I waited.

"No," he said, "I just can't."

My heart sank.

# CHAPTER
## 18

I COULDN'T SLEEP.

Half awake, my mind could see little more than a workshop full of wooden carvings and a friend of Papa's who wouldn't help me hunt horses.

Again and again, I rolled over in bed, wondering what to do, and asking myself if this trek south was little more than a kid's folly. Was it real? Or was it merely a fantasy of chasing painted ponies in a circle, a merry-go-round?

Memory was teasing me.

Over and over, I kept listening to Mrs. Skagg's old voice telling me about that horrid day, when I was two and didn't understand what was happening, and when Tate was twelve and knew only too well.

He was watching that day.

Tate had seen Gusher Plant saddle Strawberry, the red roan, perhaps knowing that Lola May Bodeen, my mother, would mount that animal only to please my father. I'd only been two, and there had been no way I could have understood the circumstances of that day, but Tate did. Tate had witnessed it all. Mrs. Skagg had stood there too, just watching, experiencing the brutal shock of my mother's death and listening to the screaming of a twelve-year-old Tate Bodeen. Perhaps we had all been too shocked to move, to help, because it happened so quickly, so unexpectedly.

Then the revenge.

My mother had been bucked off by the strawberry roan gelding, and she lay there on the Florida sand, her neck broken. Mama never heard my father's crying and never saw his genuine grief cascading down his face, and never felt the burning of his rage.

Tate saw it.

My brother, according to what Mrs. Skagg told me, must have run to his mother's side, screaming, "Mama! Mama!" But there was no responding.

Only revenge.

There was, in Tate's mind, possibly a vision of his father's anguish, and then his momentary absence. A disappearance to his barn in order to fetch his weapon of retribution.

A fullering iron.

For years, I'd seen Gusher Plant use one whenever he would reset a shoe on one of our horses. It was nothing more than a short crowbar, used for grooving and spreading iron, merely a blacksmith's tool. Yet, on this day of sadness, a fullering iron in our barn had become a cold utensil of death.

Tate saw it.

A boy of twelve had seen the uncontrolled anger of his father's returning from a barn, iron in hand, as he strode toward the corral where the red roan still stood, under an empty saddle.

My brother saw the beating.

Mrs. Skagg had confessed it to me, years later, on the evening that she had partaken too generously of the colorless liquid in the mason jar that Eli Horadoo had dropped by our place. It was intended for Gusher and Slim, but Mrs. Skagg had somehow sampled more than one pull, which had loosened her tongue.

Mrs. Skagg had seen it happen too.

The two deaths.

To her, it had been an act of unspeakable cruelty. But to Tate? As she had reported the scene to me, her hands had so often blanketed her face, as though shamed by her own remembrance.

She and my brother had watched it.

They had seen my father, Sam Bodeen, trying to cover up for his blinding lack of horse sense. They'd watched, perhaps in near disbelief, as he'd walked toward the red roan. Then the first blow. Cocking the fullering iron up over his shoulder and behind his ear, Papa had dealt the first verdict, cracking the roan's foreleg.

Closing my eyes, I could almost hear the horse's whinny of fear and agony.

A rifle or pistol could have been used. But no, because a fullering iron would be slower, and more punishing. It would take longer. I was wondering if my father had wanted the roan gelding to suffer prior to its death. Did he? How many blows had it taken? Did the roan stagger, then fall? And once the horse was down, did Sam Bodeen perpetuate the beating, blow by blow? Had my father been insane with grief over my mother's death?

When telling me, Mrs. Skagg had masked her face with both of her hands.

"Laddy, it was brutal bad. You were too young to recall it, but Tate had to see it all. Every blow of that dreadful steel. One by one, he broke the roan's legs, as though some demon had possessed his reason, and was striking with the iron."

In the big bed, at the guest room of Mr. Dodge Yardell's ranch, I rolled, then flipped my pillow over, holding my belly as though stricken with cramps.

The visions would not vacate my brain.

Yet it was difficult to imagine the frail man that I knew as my father clubbing a horse to death. But it happened. Mrs. Skagg had told me about it when I was still far too young to understand that day. In my mind, I was eager to know all the facts, yet fearful. I didn't care to envision Papa's blaming the roan gelding for his having been so pigheaded.

I could hear the horse in pain. One by one, I heard its legs breaking. It was a dreadful sound, almost beyond the borders of sanity or reason.

"Stop," I had an urge to holler.

Yet there had been no stopping Sam Bodeen. Again and again, the fullering iron struck the horse, breaking its legs, causing it finally to fall. Perhaps it had lasted less than a minute for the horse that had killed Mama. But for Tate Bodeen, it would endure forever. He had been twelve and had to watch his world being smashed and broken. His mother taken from him.

"It changed him," Mrs. Skagg had told me.

I believed her.

"Indeed, the beating and killing of that poor animal coated your brother in ice, and afterward, he was never the same child. Somehow, it froze the boy's soul. From that moment on, he was granite. He became colder than a Yankee winter. In Tate's mind, the horse hadn't killed his mother. His father had. And another thing you ought to know, Laddy. Your pa was gentle with you. But he'd never been too gentle on Tate."

These were the things Mrs. Skagg told me, years ago, before I was even old enough to balance truth against ignorance, before I could understand why Papa was the way he was, and Tate the same way.

"He adored his mother, Tate did," Mrs. Skagg had said. "So he never forgave Sam Bodeen. Nor will he. If it lasts for a hundred years, Tate will hold that day in his heart, in infamy, in some vise that has tighter jaws than any forgiveness can loosen."

I rolled over.

Eyes open in the darkness, I remembered something about that day, yet nothing definite. All I recall was the screaming of people and an animal and seeing a bleeding horse lie kicking in dusty death.

I had known who Tate was when I was two. My first spoken word had been *Tate*.

At two, I had followed the twelve-year-old giant, indoors and out, according to what Mrs. Skagg had often told me, looking up at him with wide worshiping eyes.

My remembering of the awful day was mostly fog. Swirling visions, and nothing sharp. A memory of ragged edges. Plus the noise and tears. The rage. Revenge. But these were mostly the elements that my maturity added to this bloody blending of events. Nothing of my mother's funeral could I recall. Except the hole. Her grave.

"Tate," I sighed.

I knew he would always remember Mama's burial. Did he stand there staring at the coffin, then up at Papa's face with the glowering disapproval of a twelve-year-old boy whose heart had been shattered as though by a fullering iron? Yes, I had long ago decided, Tate's mind had recorded all the facts, and the album of memory harbored all the pictures. The beautiful, and the bitter.

It was so simple to understand why Mrs. Skagg respected him. Tate was the beaten colt who somehow had survived the emotional punishment and remained sane. There really had been no burden heaped on me. All of the horror had struck my brother, on one morning, and the hammers would pound at him forever. Tate didn't forget. Or forgive. It was like our father no longer existed. Now, in Tate's mind, there was no Sam Bodeen. Only the five of us: two brothers, two hands in the bunkhouse, and Mrs. Skagg at the kitchen stove.

No daddy.

For me, I couldn't buy it.

I'd never known Mr. Sam Bodeen the tyrant. The only one I knew was a frail man, with little color on his cheeks, half-hidden under the same blanket, holding the hairbrush of a dead woman. This was all I had, however, and I hugged him every day, and talked to him, trying to say or do something that would bring him back to us, and to the Buckle Tee.

"Come back, Papa."

Thousands of times I had whispered those three words to him, hoping he'd hear, praying he would somehow respond and his long night of silence could end. "It's me, Laddy," I would tell him so often. "I'm your younger son, Tate's brother, and some-day I'll be grown up too."

He would usual only look at me from his emptiness, yet once he said my mother's name.

"Lola May," I could have sworn he said.

Upon hearing it, or imagining that I had heard it, I hadn't planned my next step. Should I have told Papa that she was dead? The one person on earth he so devotedly adored had been taken from him. Her name was that single glimmer, one solitary spark that only spent itself out, and then burrowed into a mental cavern where only Sam Bodeen could reside.

Or hide from his violence.

# CHAPTER
## 19

FINALLY I SLEPT.

But the rifle fire jolted me awake. At night, sounds are sharper, and I could hear more than one rifle barking. As I rolled out of bed, eager to discover what the excitement was outside, I could hear two different guns. The crack of each rifle had an audible personality all its own. In spite of my rodeo-sore foot, I ran to see what was happening.

Down by the corral, I found Dodge Yardell and Charlie No Water. The Seminole was naked. His chubby brown body, however, seemed to blend into the moonless night.

I saw Mr. Yardell first. He had pulled on a pair of trousers, but that was all.

Their firing stopped. Yet the acrid stench of spent gunpowder tormented my nose, and in the air, rifle smoke hung as quietly as a cattle thief.

"Want me to saddle horses?" Charlie asked his boss.

The rancher shook his head. "No. Best we wait until first light, and we'll be able to follow a clear track."

"Is somebody after your cattle?" I asked.

Mr. Yardell shook his head. "Not cattle. This particular robber never run off a single cow during his entire profession."

His remark made Charlie grin. Turning to me, the Seminole said, "It's the horses he's took. Our two mares."

I asked, "Do you know his name?"

Mr. Yardell answered. "He doesn't have a name."

Perhaps it was because I was still half asleep, but the conversation certain had twisted itself out of shape. Not wanting to sound too foolish, I didn't bother to shoo any more questions out my door. All I did was stand in the shadows and wait for what I hoped might be some forthcoming information.

Saying nothing, Charlie No Water merely walked to the shed building where he slept. Nobody said good night. I don't guess it was even partly expected.

"Show's over," Mr. Yardell said. "Until sunup."

"Is that when you and Charlie are going to track after that guy?"

"Charlie won't be going."

"You're going alone?" I asked.

"Nope." We walked side by side toward the main house. "You best come along too. It's your duty."

"Me?" I could taste last night's supper.

The man nodded. "Right, because it's that nifty little bay mare you rode in here on that's also missing."

"Brownie's gone?"

Mr. Yardell shrugged. "I'd wager she is. Along with both of my mares."

"What kind of horse thief is this man?"

"A stallion."

I could hardly breathe. But I wanted to borrow a rifle and hunt. "Is it possible that he's the stud of the band of mustangs?"

"Possible, probable, and positive."

I was wondering why Mr. Yardell didn't keep a stallion of his own to defend the mares, and I asked him how come.

"I had me one," he said, "about six months back. But that white stallion who just paid us a call hoofed him to death."

"Before I got here, I found a dead stallion, a young dapple gray, lying north of here beneath a circle of buzzards."

"Did you check his brand?" As he asked me the question, Mr. Yardell's face already suspected that I'd failed to be that curious.

"I checked. And no brand. In fact, with a bit of straining, I managed to roll the carcass over, just to look, and his dirty side was plain too." I grinned. "Are you surprised that I'd bother, Mr. Yardell?"

His hand touched my shoulder.

"Surprised and pleased." And now it seemed to be *his* turn to smile. "Good man. So suppose you shuck of the habit of calling me Mr. Yardell all the time. My name's Dodge."

A grin stretched my face. "Okay . . . Dodge."

Holding the Remington rifle in the crook of his arm, he reached inside his trouser pocket and brought out what appeared to shine like a gold watch. His thumb flicked it open. "It's coming up daylight, son. Another hour. So let's chase us up a breakfast, so we can ride out of here early and kick dust."

"Then we're going after the horses?"

"First off, boy, we're going to retake our mares. And if we happen to also round up that bonus band, we'll split fifty-fifty, the way Mr. Sam Bodeen and I used to divide it." He held out a spat-on open hand. "Equal shares?"

I shook his hand. "Equal shares."

"Let's eat, partner."

A few minutes later, we two horse hunters were busily surrounding our breakfast. Never, not once in my whole life, had a meal tasted so good. Bacon, eggs, two of yesterday's biscuits, honey, and coffee strong enough to float a horseshoe. My fork did willing chores.

"Whoa," said Dodge, "or you'll dig through the plate."

Charlie No Water, now dressed, entered the kitchen by the back door. He fried and sizzled his own breakfast and joined us at the kitchen table. Looking at me and then at his boss, he asked, "You'll take the boy?"

Dodge nodded.

"Good. That means I can stay here lonesome and tend to the ranch. If you throw a rope on that white stud," Charlie wanted to know, "you fixing to brand him?"

Dodge snorted. "I'm fixing to *shoot* him." Getting up, he busted four more eggs, two for his plate and two for mine. And I put myself outside another hot honey biscuit from the warming oven. "Eat up," he told me. "I can't haze you back home to the Buckle Tee unless we weight-gain you a pound or two." As my biscuit disappeared so sudden, Dodge boiled us some grits. "Here," he said, dumping the steamy grains on my egg-yellow plate, "do it into you."

Outside, it was still night.

Getting up from the table, Charlie No Water attacked the pots and dishes in a large pan of soapy water. Dodge and I sat at the table and let another half cup of coffee rust our pipes.

"Enjoy it," Dodge told me. "Tomorrow morning, maybe it'll be a cold camp, beef jerky, and a stale-iodine gargle of canteen water." He made a wry face. "Dang," he said, "I never thought I'd be riding out again after a band of mustangs. But I'm certain that renegade took our mares last night, along with your dancing little bay. We won't let that devil do such."

"I can't wait to go," I said. Having lost a mule, losing Brownie would be too much.

Dodge sighed. "Same here. Even though this big white patriarch may be leading the last band in Florida. Seems kind of a shame in a way. When the last mustang pokes his neck inside the loop of a rope, it'll be . . . well, it'll be final. Won't be any more to chase. Or to cuss at."

As he spoke, there seemed to be a sad note in Dodge Yardell's voice, as though he would miss having the wild stallion raiding his ranch. Yet he somehow had the itch, one final time, to wrangle some horses.

"Years back," he said, "when your daddy and I were galloping after horse dust, we saw a young white stallion leading a band of mares. We tried to corner him but he was always too foxy. Others tried too. A man named Short Callum actual swore up and down that the white we'd all been chasing, to no avail, was albino."

"It couldn't be the same stallion, could it?"

Dodge nodded. "I'd guess so. The old devil must be close to thirty years old, and still a stallion. Yes, I'd bet all my chips he's the same white stud."

Turning around from his position at the sink, Charlie No Water gestured with a soapy hand. "They live a long time, horses do."

"Well, you're right on that score, Charlie," said Dodge. "And mules live even longer, the legend goes."

I thought about our poor old Evelyn, and how quickly her life had been torn apart. "Evelyn," I said. Dodge was pouring one more swig of coffee as I said our mule's name. It caused him to turn himself around and look at me.

He said nothing for a minute, then spoke.

"In a way," he said to Charlie No Water, "I'm near to as keyed-up as the young man here, thinking about horse hunting." He winked at me. "With a saddle buddy whose name is Bodeen." Dodge let out a long sigh. "I sure wish your pa was here. We'd make a heck of a team. Sam would rather hunt horses than eat a hot meal indoors at a sit-down table served by a naked lady who could sing."

I smiled. "That's some preference."

"Your dad was a bull of a man, Laddy. A bull. A lot stronger than I ever could be. I once saw him pull a young cypress tree right up out of black muck. I'll say this for Sam. In a fight, I always wanted both of his fists on my side. Yet he wasn't what you'd honest call a forgiver. If you ever crossed him, Sam Bodeen would store away a grudge like it was folding money."

I asked Dodge to tell me more about him.

"In due time. Right now, it isn't the time for talking. We're moving, boy." Without another word, he held up two fingers, a gesture that prompted Charlie No Water to vacate the kitchen and head for the barns.

"Short Callum," he said in a low voice, "never trusted a Seminole. He was wrong. A feeling such as that is too . . . too dang absolute. I'd trust old Charlie with my life and he'd do likewise for me." Dodge shook his head. "Short was as short in nature as in stature. And he hated all Seminoles. He claimed that all they wanted to do was sneak up on white folks in the night and puncture their hides with a pointed object."

Dodge stood up. His quickness was enough to tell me that he was going to get started.

"Yes," he said, "that was Short Callum's main trouble. He was small in one-too-many ways. But I sure do miss old Short." Dodge suddenly frowned. "Well, let's not make breakfast a day's work. Not when there's horses to hunt."

Leaving the kitchen, I thought for an instant about the dead stallion I had discovered during my trip south, and what I'd seen between his teeth.

White hair.

BOOK

THREE

# CHAPTER
## 20

SUNUP CAME.

And with it, we went.

As the renegade stallion had stolen all available mares, both of us topped geldings. Dodge rode a skinny buckskin stepper that he claimed nobody could fatten, and was intended by Nature to be lean. A real rib counter, and looked as though it'd got ridden from Devil to supper without so much as a sniff of oats.

My horse was a gray gelding that had all the manners of a wild Florida boarhog. Had he been a human being, he would probable have held his dinner fork with his knuckles up. Yet, under me, the gray had a long trot he somehow stretched into miles as easy as breathing.

Dodge headed east. "Watch your horse's ears, boy," he said. "They'll tell you information. They're more useful than a pair of scouts."

Needless to say, I allowed Dodge to lead the two of us, reining my gray so that I'd trot about half a horse-length back. Close enough to talk. But not so crowding as to blind his view of left and right, because he was studying ground with our every stride.

A fox squirrel jumped us.

They are about near the size of a house cat, and my mount spooked a start that became a buck before I could rein him in and contain him. He bucked me off, quicker than a winded breath, and made me eat some Florida sand. I didn't tell Dodge how much it hurt, but it did. From up on his buckskin, Dodge looked down at me, and spat. He continued to stare as I hooked a leg up and back into the saddle. Then he gave me a short command. And a choice.

"Stick," he said, "or go home."

I stuck.

Had I been straddling Satan himself, I was intending to stay up, and not be gotten rid of. The gray tried it again. So I put a hard heel into his ribs, on one side, then turned him in about three tight circles, to let him know who was doing the riding and who was trotting.

After that, he passable behaved.

"Good seat," Dodge told me. "That gray is a range pony, and the only language he can savvy is a tight ride. No bouncing. So give it to him and he won't sorry at you anymore."

"How come," I asked Dodge, "that Charlie No Water selected this particular horse for me?"

"He wanted to see what you're made of."

Well, I was wondering, what am I made of? Today was a day of deciding. Yet I was resolved that it wouldn't be Mr. Dodge Yardell who would pass judgment on me. That, I knew, I'd handle myself. Nobody else necessary. It was going to be all Ladd Bodeen. In my wildest imagination, I couldn't envision either Sam Bodeen or Tate Bodeen ever asking anyone else whether or not they were men. They somehow knew. Now it was *my* day to prove out my manhood not to anyone. To *me*.

No one else needed to know. As long as I knew, that was the only measure that counted, and I'd prove myself to *me* and to nobody else.

Well, perhaps I'd also prove to this ornery gray between my knees that we'd be heading where I decided we'd go.

Dodge looked down. "We're hot." His hand pointed to the hoof marks in the sandy earth.

As it had turned out, Dodge Yardell's prediction had turned out to be truth. The white had run off both the D-bar-Y mares, along with my bay, Brownie. He came. And they followed. That was all there was to it. He was a dominant male that raided a ranch in the night and took all the mares he wanted. Secretly, I envied him. All he was doing was whatever Nature demanded. No more. The stallion was disobeying no law, but rather adhering to the one Law, and he was playing his part in the system.

The Creation.

As I rode behind Dodge Yardell, I wanted to be the white stallion. Whoever or whatever he was, the stud understood, and acted. In his way, his manner, he was absolute perfection, the symbol of maledom. He smelled wet mares, and then he took them, adding them all to his harem. And if a weaker stallion challenged him, woe betide weakness. Because the weakling would lie rotting underneath the Florida sun, awaiting the circling buzzards, and an army of ants.

I smiled.

God's system was severe but it worked.

In my whole life I had never been inside a church, and yet I had me an itch to attend. Mrs. Skagg had been to church, she guessed, well over a thousand times in her life, maybe even two or three thousand, and she claimed that every time had rewarded her, making her feel cleaner than soap.

"But," I had asked her as a young doubter, "does that religious feeling really last you?"

Mrs. Skagg had touched my face with a soap-fragrant hand. "No," she honestly said, "the soul cleansing *doesn't* last. But neither do a bath. Yet all us mortals now and again need one."

To her, perhaps God looked like a bar of soap. Yet what she said made a smack of sense. Mostly all of what Mrs. Skagg told me held reason, and the same for my teacher, Miss Atherton.

We rode.

Ahead of us, even though I could not actual see the band of horses, my mind could envision the stallion, a fugitive, urging his mares onward with bites and nips, and with the promise of his mating. For them, this was enough. For the mares, the entice-ment of his nearness, his smell, was sufficient to make them feel welcome to gallop at his flank. To be with him. To follow him. But I now knew that wasn't quite the way it worked.

Talking to Dodge Yardell, my knowledge about mustangs had grown more than a mite. He'd told me that a senior mare usual leads the band on a run, with the stallion in the rear, herding his mares forward by biting and sometimes by the strike of a front hoof. Mares were not led. They were driven.

"He's pushing hard," Dodge said.

I asked him why.

"He knows, or maybe suspects, that he's harvested someone's mares, so he isn't intending to tarry."

I wanted to stop.

Inside me, what seemed to be at least a half-gallon of breakfast coffee was sloshing from one kidney to the other, then invading my bladder, its pressure building and mounting until I couldn't take one more pace. The gray's trot was killing me.

"Dodge," I said, "I best empty myself."

He grinned. "Coffee?"

"Yes."

"Okay, you ride yonder, and I'll do it right here. We'll take one minute. If your bowels activate, attend it now. Later on, there might not be enough lonesome time for a fly to drop a speck."

My bowels moved.

There was no toilet paper. So, gritting my teeth, I pulled my jeans up and hoped that Mrs. Skagg would never know.

"Let's be moving," Dodge said.

"Aren't we ever going to stop?" I asked.

"Yes. Whenever *he* stops. If'n he don't, *we* don't. Remember this, that even if one or all of his mares keel over and die, he won't rest. Believe me, Laddy, he knows we're after him. He's smelled us. His nostrils have sipped the wind for information and he has learned all about us. A horse's nose can taste air like it was a whole orchestra, an entire pantry of flavor in one breezy whiff. Right now, that renegade white has discovered that there's two of us. Two human smells. That, and two strange gelding horses which cannot interest him in one sense, but can in another."

I liked hearing what Dodge was saying.

"About now," he went on to say, "the stallion knows his mares are all tuckered, yet he won't allow them to stop, sleep, or graze."

"Isn't *he* tired?"

Dodge Yardell grinned. "He's a king, boy. A *king!* And a monarch doesn't permit fatigue, not within him. His loins won't allow it. So he'll press onward until his nostrils and his ears inform him that he's outdistanced the two of us, and wore out our geldings. He won't even reward himself with a moment of romance, because he knows it could weaken him. He's intelligent. And he cannot risk the indulgence of loving because it might turn his legs to water. His legs are his life."

We rode on, heading northeast.

Between my own legs I felt a newborn manhood. I didn't feel Sue Louise. I felt Cora. And I was feeling that I was Mr. Ladd Bodeen of the Buckle Tee, a horse hunter. I was hard.

We rode about all day, turning north.

Pushing the stallion, we followed the fresh trail of hoofprints, which to me appeared to be cut by at least fifty horses. Curiously I asked Dodge how many horses we were chasing.

"Maybe a dozen. Less than a score."

"How many is a score?"

"Twenty. Don't you go to school?"

"Not very often."

Dodge grinned. "Well, you dang ought."

"Tate didn't go. In fact, at the age of twelve, he took over the running of our ranch. Now he's twenty-five, and he runs it easier than snoring."

Dodge Yardell shook his head. "Son, there's *real easy,* and there's also *looks easy.*"

"I don't understand."

"Oh, you do." He paused. "Did you ever see a juggler keep all those little clubs in the air?"

"Once, at a rodeo."

"Well, it looks easy until you try it. But then, after a number of years of practicing, it righteous becomes . . . real easy. The important thing to remember is that what's worth doing is usual hard to handle, and that *easy* never comes first." He grinned at me. "What comes first is sweat."

"You ought to see my brother Tate bronc ride. He does it more natural easier than the horse."

"I gather he's your pride."

"Sort of. I'm a ways different than Tate, yet I want to be aplenty like him."

Dodge cuffed back his hat. "Maybe," he said, "after you and I settle our business with the stallion and his band, I'd might like to visit the Buckle Tee, and meet all your people."

"Honest?"

"Yes. I could take Sam one more time."

# CHAPTER
## 21

IT WAS NIGHT.

We final stopped to rest because Dodge figured the mustangs would be stopping now, or very soon, from exhaustion.

With my head on my saddle, I was closer to sleeping than I was to the hard ground. But not my companion. Dodge was cleaning his Remington.

"You know," he told me, "there's something about house-keeping a rifle that just plain settles a man's nerves. It's about as relaxing as putting on a clean Saturday-night shirt. Or a visit to a genuine barbershop where a nose can inhale a fresh haircut. Bay Rum. That's a smell! Got such a tang to it that you don't even have to snuff both nostrils." Dodge chuckled. "I bought a bottle of Bay Rum once, and Short Callum tried to strain it through some bread slices, and then drink it."

I closed my eyes. Yet, from somewhere, I could listen up to Dodge Yardell's telling about a Saturday evening.

"As I recollect," he said, "I'd ventured into town with Short Callum. We'd run cattle for six days and neither one of us smelled any sweeter than our week-old socks. Both of us were a tight shy on crackling money, but we jingled a pocket of loose change. So old Short drank my hair tonic."

Dodge suspended his story long enough to use a pair of sticks to lift a hot no-handle coffeepot up from a low fire.

"Like I earlier said, Short Callum didn't really know a squat about cattle. But I'd give him this . . . he was a horse hunter for sure. Had himself a postage-stamp ranch, not many acres, three brood cows and a snake-horn bull. Not much of a spread. Yet enough to hunker down on and label it home."

I sighed. Listening to Dodge was better than a lullaby that Mrs. Skagg used to sing to me, years ago. Like music.

"To study at Short Callum, you'd about say that he'd be as prospering as a limp-hoof horse, and headed from nothing into nowhere. Looking at him tasted worse than patent medicine. Beside him, he always rode with a sniffer of a dog, a one-eyed bitch mongrel that Short called Lady Macbeth. Never quite could reason out the name. Short had been sweet on some lady whose name was such."

Rolling over beneath the blanket, I gave Florida my other hip.

"Short Callum," Dodge was telling me, "had hisself some strange do-daddle ways. At night, around a campfire, he'd pull out a book, then he'd hook glasses around his ears and read poetry to Sam and me." Dodge clicked his Remington together, pumping the lever into a cocking noise. "But on mules, Short didn't know the difference between a mule and a hinny."

Though I was an inch shy of sleeping, I wondered what the difference was. So I asked Dodge.

"Easy," he said. "A mule is an offspring of a jackass and a horse mare. But a hinny is the result of a union between a jennet and a stallion."

I yawned, filing all this away in my mind under the category of general ranching information.

"Cut yourself a slab of sleep," he said, "and quit all your pestering questions. We don't aim to sleep all night. Only with a lantern-light breakfast, with no lantern, because that white stallion's got hisself what you might call a travel itch."

I didn't really cotton to hear too much more about the stallion *or* Short Callum, not now, because the curtain of sleep was starting to lower all around me, and the world was a silent bed. My eyes were closing shut.

How long I had slept was a mystery.

All I now knew was that Dodge Yardell was shaking me awake, telling me to pull on my boots and throw the blanket and saddle over the spine of a gray gelding. Opening one eye, I could see no light, and also make out that Dodge wasn't fixing to do a breakfast. As I stumbled to where my gray was tethered, I could smell oats on his breath, so Dodge had made sure our horses had eaten a meal. For us, however, it would be a feedbag full of oxygen and little else.

"What time is it?"

Dodge snorted. "How in the deuce do *you* care? You're not going to attend a social, are you?"

"No, I don't guess so."

Rubbing my eyes, I could see that Dodge was already mounted, high up on his skinny buckskin. The rib counter. Reins in his left hand, he circled the gelding a turn or two, as if to inform me that he was impatient to move out and ride.

"Well," he said, his voice softening somewhat, "if you really got to know the time, it's closing in on three o'clock in the morning."

I moaned. "It's still night."

"Maybe so," Dodge told me, "but that white stud horse just might be thinking different. I sort of took myself a fearful notion that he's nuzzled his mares awake and given all them their parading orders."

"How do you know that?"

"I don't." Dodge wheeled his horse once again. "Just a hunch. Maybe the old patriarch has decided that he'll outsmart us and steal a march before first light. He done that to your pa, Short, and me more'n once. That scoundrel's been outsmarting half of Florida for close to three decades."

For some reason, the cinch strap on my saddle wasn't tightening, so I pulled harder. It should have moved to a snug, yet it didn't. Maybe the gray was inflating his stomach, to ease the pressure, so that the saddle would cinch up too loose.

"Knee him," Dodge told me.

I didn't understand. "What?"

"Bring your knee up, really hard, and knock a heave of wind out of him. Or else he'll do you like this every time he feels a saddle to his backbone."

I kneed him.

"Harder. That wouldn't deflate a bull butterfly."

Jacking up my knee with all my force, I knew pronto I'd leastwise gotten the animal's attention. He expelled air from both ends. The backside air was a lot less than fragrant.

"Good. Now hitch up that cinch strap so he's realizing that you mean business, and it ain't Sunday."

I mounted up.

Dodge clucked to his bony buckskin, and we were off. Hard telling exactly what direction. The old gent's nose was tasting the night air, and I could see his hatchet face beneath the brim of his hat, splitting the wind like it was kindling. He rode, and I rode. There wasn't much of a moon because of cloud cover, and in less than an hour, it rained. A typical Florida summer downpour, with lightning and thunder, and it forced us to unroll our slickers.

Dodge spurred the rib counter from an easy trot to an eager mud-flinging canter.

I reasoned why.

The rain, coming down now as determined as it was, could rinse away the hoofprints, and then all we'd be following would be mud and guesswork.

We rode for what I figured to be over ten miles. My stomach wanted breakfast, yet I certain didn't dare mention my yearnings to Dodge Yardell.

The rain continued.

It was a wetting that no slicker could keep out, and I was beginning to feel like a fish in search of a frypan, not to mention hungry, tired, and willing to whoa. Right now, I was thinking, a fire would feel precious good. A campfire, coffee, and a roll up into slumber. Or maybe a giant mug of steaming tea. And a hot biscuit. As the rain let up, the sun in the east began to squint at us through the distant cabbage palms.

Dodge reined in.

"Easy."

His one word confused me. Nothing about this nighttime ride had resembled *easy*. But I held myself quiet and waited for the old gentleman to explain. He did.

"Up ahead," he told me in a whisper.

Looking, I saw next to nothing.

Pulling the Remington from its saddle scabbard, Dodge held the reins in his teeth while he lever-cocked his rifle. I wondered if Dodge had seen the white stud and was intending to smack a bullet into him. Watching him yank the brim of his Stetson a half inch closer to his eyes, I had little doubt.

"We're close," he again whispered.

"How can you tell?"

"I can't. Not for certain. But the horse smell is out there. It's only a feeling a man gets in his belly, a sense that there's a wild band nearby, and it's time to hit 'em."

"You're going to shoot him?"

"Honest am."

"Why don't we capture the whole lot?"

"Because."

The one-word explanation reminded me of my brother. Tate Bodeen explained matters in the same way, as though too impatient to outline the obvious to simpletons who couldn't savvy it. Or, same thing, to a kid brother. Well, I'd just stitch my lips together and learn how it was done, even though I really didn't hanker to watch any animal stop a bullet and meet his death. Even the stallion. Leastwise, not until I'd seen him live a spell.

The dawn strengthened.

"Boy," Dodge said at last, "they're up ahead for certain. And they're resting." The old man shook his head very slowly, a sad gesture. "Strange," he said, "but five or six years ago, that stallion wouldn't have stopped to rest. He'd have pushed further and lost us. I wonder if he realizes that he's growing old, like me. Short Callum's dead, and that pesky stud horse will go next." He sighed. "It all sort of slips away in the night."

Dodge pointed.

"There."

I looked.

Sure enough, I could see a horse band, no larger than specks, grazing on our side of a stand of pines, about a mile distant. The feeling in Dodge Yardell's belly had paid off. It was real. The horses were all there. Waiting. And I wondered if the stallion knew we were here and yet felt too old to escape.

"Can he see us, Dodge?"

"Only if we move. Or shout. Right now, we are downwind of him, and that's exact where we'll remain put."

"What do we do now?"

"Quit asking."

I kept mute. If Dodge wanted me to know something, he'd probable bust out and inform me. But if not, then I'd think it all out for myself. His brain wasn't the only. I could reason too.

The hush of early morning, like night, still lay asleep all around us. There was a misty fog that rolled along tight to the ground, in low clouds, and I welcomed the silence. It was like I was watching God awaken, stretch, and crank up a day.

Dodge dismounted slowly. His right leg hooked back over the cantle, moving like a swamp heron stalking a frog. Hardly a motion at all.

"Fall off," he told me. "Slow."

I did.

Standing directly behind him, I could see the fuzzy outline of his body. His legs seemed unfit for walking, so bowed that they appeared to be straddling a ghost horse or a valentine. My mind kept on serpentining around questions, yet avoiding each one, as a downhill crick dodges around rocks. Turning to me, Dodge cleared up the matter of what we'd do next.

"Now," he said, "we'd best crawl."

# CHAPTER
## 22

"CRAWL?"

The man nodded. "To be a horse hunter," he whispered, "is to realize that the final mile is the hardest. The slowest, and yet exciting enough to chatter your teeth like a collie dog."

"You really aren't going to use your Remington on the stud horse." I paused, hoping he'd disagree. "Are you?"

Dodge gestured with his rifle. "Laddy, for a long time, I've had me an ache to finish that hunk of dog meat. A number of years now, he's run off my mares, or tried to, and that dang outlaw has always kept himself and his band one jump ahead of me." He patted the rifle stock. "Today might be my day."

Right then, I wanted to tell Dodge that I'd come to Republic Flat to hunt horses, not to shoot them. But at first I held quiet. Mr. Dodge Yardell didn't look like a man who'd be too anxious to solicit my opinion. Inside, I knew that *my* opinion was the only one that really counted, not Dodge's. Or not Tate's. So I decided it was time to stand straight up, in a sense, and speak my mind.

"No," I said firmly.

He looked my way. "No what?"

"Don't destroy the stud horse."

Dodge inhaled, and then sighed. "Boy, he's captured your bay mare. I would figure that you might want to reclaim her."

"I do."

"Well then, let's have at it," he said.

"We ought to take the band alive."

Cuffing back his hat, the old man stared through me until I was suspecting that he disremembered how to talk. Then he final spoke up.

"Don't you think that stallion'll have himself some ideas about getting took? You can't figure that he's going to stroll into a corral, close the gate, latch it, announce that he's our property, and then brand himself."

"I don't guess he'll do such, no," I said, realizing at once that I was speaking up too loud.

Dodge leaned against the trunk of a pine. "Let's keep our voices low," he said, "in spite we both got a couple of strong feelings about matters."

"Okay," I whispered.

"I thought you hankered to be a horse hunter."

I nodded. "That's the truth, sir. I do. But I wasn't counting on becoming a horse *killer,* that's all." Inside, I was fighting an image of Sam Bodeen and a fullering iron, beating a red roan gelding to death. But I couldn't tell Dodge Yardell about it. I was hoping that his opinion of Papa was shining, so it made no sense to throw mud on this old gentleman's memory. In a way, I was protecting both Dodge and Papa, yet I had to do it private. Some happenings in my life were too deep beneath my skin to talk about, even with Mrs. Skagg.

Dodge spat.

"So our young Mr. Ladd Bodeen isn't a horse killer. Well, to give you the straight of it, neither am I." He paused. "Maybe it took a youngster who recent rode my wooden ponies, smiling like he couldn't ever quit, to force me to realize that I guess I'd rather build than destroy."

"Never figured you did," I said. "Your horse carving's too handsome to allow you to do sorry."

As I spoke, I was thinking about my brother, and how his watching Papa's beating a horse to death had turned him so cold. It wasn't Tate's fault. He'd only been a kid at the time. Tate was like the green colt that Dodge and I gentled two days ago. My brother had been quirted across the eyes by a sight no boy of twelve should rightly have to witness on the same day his mother had been bucked off and killed.

I looked at Dodge. "Maybe," I said, "the two of us could somehow gentle that renegade."

The man chuckled. "Boy," he said, "I'll have to salute your gumption. You certain ain't modest when it comes to setting yourself a goal."

A vision of Cora Blike and her little baby boy, Burlin, crept softly into my mind. It turned me into joyful, so happy that I felt the corners of my mouth rising. Happier, when I made my next statement to Dodge.

"The stallion," I said, "isn't the most important mission in my life. Come to think about it, he's nowhere near at the top of my list."

Dodge Yardell shook his head.

"Yessir," he said in his soft voice, "you sure are Sam Bodeen's colt, even though maybe you yourself have yet to discover it." Walking to where I stood, Dodge gave my shoulder a very gentle punch. "There was a pinch of goodness in your father. Oh, he did his level hardest to hide it, clenched inside his fist, and the very few of us horse hunters who rode with him never let on to Sam we knew his tender streak existed. His gentle underbelly.

But it was always there, cropping up in Sam when we'd least expect it to blossom." Dodge nodded slowly. "Somewhere," he said, "inside of Sam Bodeen there was a flower seed."

"I know," I told him. "He's my father. And for me, he doesn't have to be faultless. Only human."

"All right, we said enough for now. I'm not growing any younger," Dodge admitted, "and that band of mustangs won't draw any closer. Let's go hunt us some horses."

"Alive?"

Dodge nodded. "Alive and kicking."

"We'll need an enclosure, won't we?"

"Eventual. But out here, Laddy, there isn't much of a purpose to corral them, and then set on a fence rail to cogitate what we're fixing to do next." He looked at me. "You got any manner of plan?" Dodge asked, as if he already had one.

"Yes," I said, "we corner the whole band and settle between us which ones are yours and which are mine. Then we brand 'em, and that's that." An amusing thought struck me, so I spoke it right out. "My guess is, you'd like that stallion for yourself."

"Me? That heller?"

"The two of you have fought over this turf too long to be strangers."

"I'll be hanged," Dodge said, cuffing back his hat.

"What's the trouble?"

"Boy, you discovered my soft spot."

"So you want the stallion?"

He nodded. "Yes, I sort of do."

"Good."

"That stud is a challenge," Dodge said. "I'd never dream of attempting to domesticate him, or effort to turn him into a house cat. He's not the breed of animal that'll ever jump up into my lap and purr. Yet I'd sort of cotton to the idea of having the old fellow around, so's the brace of us could ripen old together."

As he spoke, Dodge squinted to the north, his leathery face softening to a slightly sentimental expression.

"Over the years," he said, "he's taken mares from me, and I've stolen mares from him. Back and forth, we have raided one another's stock. Both that old stallion and I have been horse hunters. In a way, I was a mite grateful that Sam Bodeen wasn't here to play in on all of it. That there stallion and Sam would've killed each other. No Florida range could have held the two of them peaceful."

"Okay, you get the stud."

"Agreed," he said.

"Well, you're the boss. What's our next move?"

He scratched his ruddy neck, the deeply-lined skin just above his collar and below his gray hair. "North of here," Dodge said, "there used to be an old corral on a deserted land claim. In the past, Short Callum and your daddy and I employed it on round-ups, and there's no cause that it's gone off. Here and there, it'll might require some repair work. We can patch in a rail, if need. There's also a shed."

"Sounds like sense."

"All right, we don't crawl," Dodge said. "And it suits me nifty, on account I'm too weary to creep much further than from here to the rib counter." He pointed to his gelding. "But we best mount up and push those mustangs a tad more. They'll drive easier when they're tired. The stud will travel just far enough to lose sight of us, yet not so distant to fade us away complete."

"Couldn't we rest an hour?"

Dodge pushed me toward my horse. "We could rest forever, not catch a single animal, and you'll return home with a bucket of squat. Is that to your liking, Mr. Horse Hunter?"

"No," I said, my eyes sagging.

"Mount up," he said.

"How about half-an-hour snooze?"

Dodge grunted. "Laddy, when you're *my* age you can rest. That's what we old farters do all day. If'n you doubt me, then go ask Charlie No Water. Some days, the pair of us don't accomplish much more than breakfast and supper, but not a lick in between, except a nap to rest up before bedtime."

Standing beside his horse, he stared at me as though wondering whether or not I possessed the bowels to keep on tracking. So I kicked up into the saddle. "Ready," I told him.

"Good lad."

"When does the stallion sleep?"

Dodge grabbed his horse's reins and twirled them a turn or two. "Oh, whenever he reasons he's lost the hunters who are after him. But you can bet he won't ever lie down. All he'll do is lock his knees and allow his head to droop a few inches. However, his ears will be up, and alert, savoring every little noise like it was music.

He stared down at his Remington.

As he did so, I was wondering what thoughts were now passing through his mind. I doubted that he was thinking about resting. But perhaps I was wrong. For a moment I felt ashamed that the old gentleman could sport more stamina than I. Well, I swore that I'd keep up with him, even if we rode all day long and took a bite out of evening. I'd take everything this chase could dish out. Yet it might be more than decent if Mr. Dodge Yardell would consider our having a gnaw or two.

"You hungry?" he asked me as if guessing.

"Nope, not me." My stomach was yelping. And I even heard an echo in its emptiness.

"Let's eat a bite," he said, "then we'll continue to crowd that white rebel and grind his hoofs off." He shoved the rifle into a holder, barrel back and butt forward, ahead of the right skirt of his saddle. Smiling, he turned to me. "I don't guess we'll be using the Remington."

It was good to hear.

## CHAPTER
## 23

WE ATE.

Then we rode.

"He's circling," Dodge told me.

I was near to half asleep, maybe more, and my head jolted up. Luckily I didn't tumble out of the saddle.

"Yep, that old Romeo is heading to the northwest. Can't say I'm surprised," Dodge said. "One thing I learned as a horse hunter, years ago, and that's this. A band of mustangs will roam in one giant circle." He shot a smile at me. "In a sense, son, they're akin to wooden ponies on a merry-go-round. Except with wild horses, their circle is considerable larger. Yet they keep roaming the same turf, around and around a hub, like they're hearing some silent waltz-time calliope."

"That's good," I said in a daze.

"You sleepy yet?" he asked.

My head jerked up, faking that I was still awake and listening up. "Circle," I said, resuming my slump.

"Whoa."

"Are we going to stop?"

"Boy, you've been stopped for ten miles. Maybe more closer to twenty. Kick off that horse before you spill."

I dismounted.

"Good. Now loosen the cinch, pull off the saddle and bridle, and then rub him until he's bone-dry. Hear?"

"Yessir." I wouldn't have needed all that obvious advice had I been awake.

"Hobble him. No sense our tracking double on account you lost your animal." Dodge yawned. "I best admit I'm a inch to the weary side myself."

The wind was right.

So, building a small fire, Dodge boiled us tea and fried us some grub, in less time than to ask him when we'd ever point our fangs at food again. The chuck was hot, brown, and plentiful. It didn't take me long to shovel it all into me until my gut burned with hot beans.

"Dodge," I asked, "did Papa really have a softer side to his nature?"

He glanced at me. "Does it matter?"

"Yes. A lot."

He took a sip of tea. "Well, one time your father and Short Callum and I were visitors at a place called the Hawk and Spit, which was sort of a heehaw house."

"What's that?"

Staring at me for a moment, he said, "It's a commercial estab-lishment that features rainbow-faced ladies who merchandise what a gentleman might call horizontal diversion. So, to git along my story, seems there was a cardsharp in there that a bunch of cowpokes were picking on, because he was so ladyish. His name, as I recall, was Michael McGee, and he was as dandy a fancy Irisher as you'd ever expect to meet. He possible wore lace-curtain undies. Smelled like perfume. Perfect hair. And his prissy walk would make the Army lose interest. Anyhow, some waddy lost a poke of money to Miss Michael, as he often got called, and turned sour about it. He even lined up two of his pals, as if one little slap wouldn't spook Mike into a spasm. Ganged up, you might say. Nobody did a thing to prevent it, save for one man. Your pa."

"My father?"

"That's correct. Even though both of us were loaded, Short Callum and I witnessed the whole shebang. Your daddy stepped forward and slugged a bully or two, and then asked Michael McGee to join him in a drink. Nobody dared even to hawk or spit, as only fools stood up against Sam Bodeen. He was the single gentleman in that saloon who as much as announced he'd be that faggot's friend. That was Sam's softness. His flower seed. Aside from his tough and unruly ways, it was that smack of goodness that made him worth knowing, and riding alongside Short and me."

Awake now, I said, "I'm glad you told me."

"So am I." Dodge threw a twig at me in a friendly way. "And I'm really glad about my coming along with you, Ladd. It sort of takes me backward a score and a half of years, to when your pa and I rode together. We had our fights. One was a rip snorter. Yet I'm still grateful that I knew your pa."

"Me too," I said quietly, eyes closed.

I slept for a spell.

Waking up, I saw Dodge, already up and on his feet, boots on, looking to the northwest through a telescope. He collapsed it with a series of three tiny clicks, and stuffed the telescope into his saddlebag.

"Ladd," he said, "we best skirt around the band, and go check on the corral. If my memory serves, it's up ahead, a comfort lot closer than I first suspected. But it'll do. So shake yourself up and slap some leather on that gelding, and we're off to the northwest."

As I was doing what I'd been told, I asked Dodge exactly where this old corral was located.

"Near a place called Confederation." He looked at me for a second or two. "I'd wager you rode right on through it on your way south from where you got so nocturnal cozy with young Miss Cora."

I sat up. "Cora Blike?"

"That's the very young lady I'm mentioning."

"We're close to where she's at?"

Dodge grinned. "About twenty hollers and ten spits."

My heart leaped. "I'm awake."

"So help me, Hannah," the old gentleman told me, "if you plant another baby in that child's belly, I will personal boot your butt from Hell to breakfast. You're too fine a boy to steal your pleasuring at the risk of her poverty."

I stood up. "Hold on. I'm not the father of Burlin, if that's what you're thinking. Who he is happens to be nobody's business. I won't trespass Cora. So it's high time you quit hounding me on the subject. I got decency of my own without your advice, and it happens to be the only decent I can rely on. I don't need a wet nurse when it comes down to having some proper behavior." I planted both fists on my hips. "So drop it."

Dodge smiled. "Consider it dropped and busted."

My voice quieted down a turn or two. "Thanks for caring about her. Maybe not enough people have, so I appreciate your horning in. But I don't aim to listen up to a pointing finger, when all your guesswork isn't true. Hear?"

"I hear." Dodge shook his head. "You sure are feisty about Miss Cora, and maybe I'm certain glad you be. And you're commencing to sound more like old Mr. Sam Bodeen with every breath."

I smiled. "Well, I'm not my pa. But it's okay with me if I sound like him."

We rode.

"This'n a gamble," Dodge muttered.

"How so?"

"We're sort of banking on that stallion's leading his mares to us, completing the circle," Dodge said. I could almost hear him thinking. "You claim you discovered a dead stallion up this way. Well, that's on the track. Men who murder, as the saying goes, return to the scene of the crime. So it is with horses. A path is a friend to an animal, a trusted pal. It'll lead to water, to food, to a proven resting place. Talking to trappers, I've learned that much. That is exact how they set and bait their leg-holders. Along a path."

"So that's what we're doing?"

"Yessir, my boy. That's it. We're ahead of him now. He thinks we're still behind him, that stallion do. We won't be for long. You and I, son, are away ahead of that hellion, and we'll now permit him to come to us. Simple as pigs."

Sure enough, we arrived at an old cordon, almost entirely enclosed by thick brush, where the wooden rails and posts were graying with age, like a gathering of old people. The posts hadn't been cut of cedar, no creosote, and no Tate Bodeen to demand their enduring. It made me miss Tate. Perhaps he didn't miss me a whole bunch, but I didn't care, because he'd soon know he had Mr. Ladd Bodeen for a brother.

Inside the corral Dodge dismounted, bent over, and examined the dirt. "Hoof marks," he said softly. "Old ones."

"Shod?"

"No, not a sign of iron. And there's a lot of manure, all of it old, which'll tell us that the mustangs have used this enclosure to hide in during a daytime. All we have to do is sweeten the pot. We'll bait the trap with some carrots and oats, crushed into a mash, and it'll be enough to make a hungry horse tuck a napkin under his chin."

Considering the fact that we worked so earnestly it didn't take us long to do the patching work. A rail here, and a post over yonder. We were lucky the surrounding brush would thicken and heighten the fence. Luckily, Dodge had brought along a small hatchet, and nearby was a stand of scrub live oak. A day's labor finished the job, but it certain was a full and long day.

Later he shot a possum.

After sundown, because the wind was allowing, we roasted it over a low ground fire and it tasted near as good as chicken. A mite more greasy. On top of possum we had grits, onions, potatoes, and some funny doodad biscuits that Dodge rolled out of salt, sugar, flour dough, baking powder, and baked brown on a stick.

"What's it called?" I asked Dodge behind a full mouth.

"Twist," he said.

"It'd be even better under butter."

Dodge chuckled. "Right, so you go fetch us a milk cow and a churn, not to mention the waiting for her milk to curdle, and we'll do butter."

Wow, I certain was tired again. The ache of work was nagging all my bones and bruises.

Near the old corral there was a shed. Not much of a shelter, but a lot more roof than a slicker, in case it rained. And rain it did. Not drops. Buckets. It reminded me of the night at Cora Blike's place when I was sopped clear to bone, and chilly, and she rubbed me near to raw with her chigger-free blanket, not caring that I was newborn-naked.

With my head on a saddle, I was closing in on sleep. Sleep! What a beautiful word. A silent sound, one that crept up on you and kissed your cheek, tucking you in. Sleep.

"Indeed," said Dodge.

I couldn't quite reason out what he was muttering about, or why, and I didn't care a whit.

"He was indeed a man, your old pa."

Eyes closed, my mouth smiled.

It sounded right pleasant to hear somebody talk nice about my father. At school, some of the kids didn't do such, and often badmouthed him to my face. Tate wondered why I came home from school, a lot of times, with a puffy lip and a mouth scab. There wasn't any purpose telling him. He wouldn't have understood. I did understand, because crazy Mr. Sam Bodeen happened to be my father. But my brother would eye my bruises and then ask his usual question.

"How come you never lick anybody, Lady?"

In my sleep, I could hear his hardening voice asking the question to me, as though I wasn't more than another Michael McGee in Irish-lace underwear. Not once, never, did I tell Tate that I'd fought at school defending our daddy and his reputation.

Oh, it was easy, now that Mr. Sam Bodeen was a silent cripple, easy to stand up to him from a distance. But when he was in prime, how many of them would have stood against him, toe to toe, and fist against fist? Not a one, I'd wager. Yet, after his illness, it was so courageous for the cowards of the village to kick a dead lion. Back when the lion roared, none would have been able to work up the gumption to face him, eye to eye.

I felt really confused, wondering exactly where our family was headed. We were something like a crick, serpentining around the higher places, not knowing where it flowed. Only down.

"Yes," said Dodge, "Sam was a real man. Yet sometimes he'd turn even too ornery for jail."

# CHAPTER
## 24

"WAKE UP."

Opening my eyes, I could see little except moonlight, and Dodge who was shaking me by the shoulder.

"Ladd, keep alert."

"What's . . . happening?"

"Nothing yet. But I suspicion he's coming."

"Who?"

"The dang Easter Bunny," Dodge grumbled. "Git up to your feet, pull your boots on, and abide patient. Because I can smell horses as sure as the Good Lord put pits in cherries."

Earlier, Dodge and I had baited the cordon with oats and crushed carrots, rubbing the pulp on fence posts and rails. It was, he said again, a smell that would lure the wariest of horses. Like ice cream for a child.

Nearby, a narrow crick had become plump from all the fresh rain. So the elements were there. Oats. Water. Carrots. Soon the mustangs would come in the night and belong to us. I'd get back my Brownie mare. We opened the small gate, one that was no more than ten feet in length.

Our trap was baited and ready.

While we waited, Dodge smeared the two of us with dabs of

his oaty carrot tincture. "There," he said, smelling his own hand. "This'll mask the human stink of us."

"We don't stink."

"To a horse, we do, son. Maybe to lots of wild animals. A human being's got a strong scent, and I'd imagine in a mustang's nostrils we smell close to dirt, danger, or damnation."

We waited.

The combined oats and carrots were starting to distress me. "If we didn't stink before," I whispered to Dodge, "we sure as certain do now. I smell like a salad."

"Good. You're part of our hookworm."

Dodge had been thorough in his baiting preparation. Inside the cordon, he'd also hobbled our two geldings, as if to invite the stray band to enter. Dodge said that the geldings might appear, in the night, to be a pair of mares. Geldings, unlike mares and studs, have almost no scent at all. Later, the stallion would ignore their presence, as a gelding was docile and presented no threat to his authority.

My eyes sagged.

Yet my hand never once let loose its hold on the open gate, behind the blind of pine boughs where we were hidden. This night, I truly felt, would be a time in my life that I would always remember, and keepsake it. It was my first horse hunt. Sadly, it was also perhaps the last horse hunt for Mr. Dodge Yardell. Even sadder, maybe this was the last wild band of horses in Florida, as Dodge worried it might be.

"You awake?" Dodge was whispering.

"Yes."

"Good, because we have company."

"They're coming!"

"Hush. Hold quiet, or you'll spook 'em." His hand covered my mouth to silence me.

I held quiet. Neither of us said another word for, I guess, over an hour. Then, even though the moon had hidden too, I thought I detected a slight movement, about a hundred yards away. Then another.

"It's the mares," Dodge whispered, close to my ear. "They'll enter the corral first. Don't worry, the stud will be the final. He'll bring up the behind, the tail end. It's not cowardice on his part but Nature's way. And it makes good reason, the way all the Creation do."

One by each, the mares approached the gate.

A mare nickered. She was answered by one of our geldings, Dodge's, as though he was telling her that she and her sisters would be welcome inside the enclosure, and to parade right in. I could have kissed that skinny rib counter right on the muzzle, as he was doing what neither Dodge nor I could do. Yet I had to credit Mr. Yardell's foxy wisdom. Perhaps he'd counted on more than ribs. The old horse hunter had known that an audible exchange might be possible, and it was. I began to wonder if Dodge was the world's smartest person.

Step by step, they came. My heart leaped as I spotted the return of my bay, Brownie.

Ears up, the mares came toward our cordon until I counted seven. No more than that. I had hoped for a score. Twenty. But all I could add up was seven. While six waited, one mare would advance our way, then stop, and wait for all of the other six to move. It was so darn pretty to behold that it took all my discipline to hold back whooping. One by one, the mares entered the gate, heads high, ears up and forward, advancing to the far side to join the geldings. Horses, I'd learned, like being with other horses. So the nine of them, seven mares and our two geldings, slowly banded together as drops of water unite into a puddle.

We saw the natural flow of life.

"Where's the stud?" I breathed.

Dodge, beside me, placed a finger to his lips. "He'll be along. Wait patient. It could take his majesty another hour before he's convinced that the corral is to his liking." He paused. "If you're real itchy, we could close the gate now and settle for only the mares."

"No," I said, "you deserve the stallion." I smiled. "And he deserves to know you."

"We could fumble the whole band, Laddy."

"Okay, so we could. But let's chance it, because I think he'll come, Dodge, I honest do." I took a deep breath. "I know, my mare's returned, and I'm risking losing her again. But I want you to have the stallion and to try to gentle him. And give him a name."

I saw his teeth grin. "Laddy, in the past thirty years, I've called that raider every dang *name* I could think of."

We waited.

Minutes went by, a whole lot of them.

Then I spotted a light shape moving our way, a ghost, coming toward the open gate. The stallion! Head high, he expanded his nostrils, testing the wind. One of his mares called to him, yet he refused to answer her. As he walked closer, very cautiously, I could see the scars and the welts on his massive body, wounds of when he'd been bitten and kicked, fighting to preserve his females, his life, and his empire.

I knew why Dodge Yardell wanted him.

He was worthy of wanting. The stud was powerful, stately, moving as though he knew who he was, a monarch, a free ruler. A king. Tossing his head, he seemed to be announcing that he was royalty.

A mare again called to him from inside our corral. An invitational sound.

This time, he answered her with a lower-pitched fluttering

call. It came from deep in his throat, as if to assure her that everything was all right, and that he'd be joining the band in his own casual time. His hoofs never seemed to stop prancing.

At the gate, he stopped. He smelled something foreign, not part of his native Florida outback. As his white body tensed, I could feel the power of his legs and haunches. His hind hoofs pounded the earth. Again at the gate, he balked, shying away, even though his desire was to join the mares inside the circular corral.

Earlier, Dodge and I had checked every post, each railing, making sure that all lengths of wood could withstand the charge of horses who suddenly realized they were no longer at liberty.

Wheeling, the stallion bolted away, and my heart about sank into both of my boots.

We lost him.

But he thundered away for thirty or forty feet, no more, wheeling around again as abruptly as he had departed. Back to the gate he danced, hoofs kicking the earth, every hoof hammering into the Florida muck as if punctuating the heavy statements of his maledom. He was mature, but still a stallion.

Entirely male.

Again he galloped a rope length away, and I heard Dodge Yardell's confident voice whisper one word. "Steady."

I couldn't answer. Or speak. I'd let Dodge and his velvety voice handle most of our conversation, and right now, all of our thinking. Watching the stallion trying to make up his mind was all I could handle for the moment. Once more, the white sachem returned to the gate, muttering, shaking his head from side to side as though inside his mind some infernal debate was raging, confounding him, testing his reason and judgment.

He reared.

As if pumping the pedals of an unseen bicycle, with forelegs striking high in the air, the stud stood on hindquarters, pawing the night, or a celestial enemy. Coming down, his front hoofs were inside the gate, yet again he retreated a yard or two, unwilling to commit his freedom to the baited enclosures that now contained his mares, plus our pair of geldings.

Then, with a decisive toss of his head and mane, the stallion trotted forward to join his band of mares at the far end, fifty yards inside the gate. He was satisfied. There was no danger, no risk of capture, the corral was a previously used haven of safety upon which he and his band could now rely, and trust.

"Now," said Dodge.

We slid the gate into place, closing the cordon, imprisoning our prizes. I snugged the rawhide thong over the key post.

"We got 'em," I told Dodge.

Luckily, we had reinforced the gate itself to strengthen it, double strong. A good thing, because the stallion came like a train, his chest crashing into the pair of upper rails, and I heard the wood crack. He let out a whinny, a cry so human, so filled with fear and regret, as though confessing to the entire world his stupidity.

We had prepared. Quickly we added a strong pole of twelve feet to reinforce the gate's crest. It was thick and strong.

Meanwhile, the mares were cantering in circles around the inside perimeter of the corral, a fence too high to jump, as though expecting an escape route to be found. The white male, following his initial charge into the hard resisting wood, did not gallop. Instead, he stood silently, facing us, as if to tell his mares that there was no escape. Only capture.

The stallion knew.

# CHAPTER
## 25

WE STOOD OUTSIDE THE CORDON.

Resting our hands and forearms on the upper rail of the gate, Dodge Yardell and I observed our captured band. Only our two hobbled geldings looked reasonable calm. The rest were still milling, including my bay and the other two mares belonging to Dodge.

"Wow," I said. "We did it."

Stretching out a hand, Dodge messed up my hair. "But," he warned, "it's a tad like grabbing a tiger by the tail." He glanced at me. "What do we do now with all of our prizes? Any ideas, Laddy?"

It was still totally night.

"Well," I said, "I ought to pack myself off to sleep. But I don't guess I can sleep for even a wink, on account I'm so excited and churned up."

Dodge grinned. "Yup, me too." He paused. "How I'm wishing that your pa and Short Callum were here, to see this."

I agreed. "But I s'pose the first thing we ought to do is collect our domestics and ease all of them out of the corral, away from the wild stock."

Dodge shook his head. "Wrong."

"How so?"

"Because it will help settle the wild horses down, to be amongst tame. You'll see. I read that in a book one time, about elephants in India. Whenever they capture a fresh wild one, the Hindu people put him amongst the elephants already tame, so's he'll gentle down to helpful in a hurry."

"Is that true?"

"Seems to me it be. Make sense to you?"

I thought about it. "Reckon it does. The India people know about such matters; the same way you likewise know horses, they know elephants."

"After a while," said Dodge, "we've got to visit a meadow and cut some hay for these animals. Right now, however, best we starve them some."

"Why?"

"It'll serve to docile 'em. Weaken them a kick or two. Not too serious. Yet enough to allow hunger to pat a steadying hand along their backs, so when we return with fodder, they'll welcome us warm. We'll let them connect us with chow."

So much of whatever Dodge said held reason that it seemed to me like he invented logic. I wanted him to meet Miss Atherton, my teacher. She was logical too.

"Maybe," I said, "I'll turn in. Right now, I'm so doggone sleepy that I could doze off with my cheekbone on this here fence and consider it a pillow." I turned to Dodge. "Are you turning in too?"

"No." He shook his head. "I figure I'll stay up a spell and talk to my white friend in there. We never met face to face before. But we're far from strangers, because I know his smell and he knows mine. I'd just take pleasure in striking up a conversation with him. Maybe we'll forgive each other."

I went to lie down in the shelter.

Eyes open, I lay there with my head on a saddle, unable to sleep. Inside, my stomach was still spinning around like a buzz saw. Closing my eyes, I could see nothing except a cordon with horses in it, two geldings, seven mares, and the magnificent stud. Sleep was impossible. So I got up, took a trip to the crick, and scrubbed most of the oaty carrot smell off me.

Above, there was a moon.

"Cora," I said to it.

Strolling out by the corral, I spotted Dodge at the fence gate, one boot resting easy on a bottom rail. And I could hear his smooth voice, as I moved closer, talking to the stallion. Would an old man and an old stud horse, traditional enemies, become eventual friends?

If anyone could gentle that wild stallion, without cutting all the male off him, Dodge was the gentleman.

It wasn't my intention to eavesdrop, or to spy. Yet I couldn't help but overhear what he was saying over the fence to the stallion. "All right now, old fellow . . . I'm not about to hurt you, or to take away all of your fair company. So don't toss your proud head up so high and roll your eyes at me thataway. I'd wager, in horse years, you're even older than I am, so maybe you and I and Charlie No Water can rest out our days at the D-bar-Y. Would you care to do that? I hope so, because Charlie and I would consider it an honor to invite you to be our guest. Carrots and oats included free."

Hearing him talking, I knew why people brought their troublesome horses to Dodge Yardell. He ought, I was thinking, do such for children too. To be sure, he'd already settled me some, and I was beginning to feel that I knew who I was. Mr. Ladd Bodeen of the Buckle Tee.

"I like it," I said, "being *me.*"

Dodge turned around to see me coming his way. "S'matter," he asked, "can't you snore?"

"Too excited," I told him, "like those milling horses in there. Maybe I just might have more important matters on my mind, besides horses."

With a thumb, Dodge lifted the brim of his hat, as though wanting to help himself to a keener look at me. "If you'd oblige me a wild guess," he said, "I would say it might point in the direction of Miss Cora."

"Smack on the money."

"Tomorrow," he said, "you might consider riding over to her place and then fetching her to here, to see our captives."

My heart leaped.

"I'll leave right after breakfast."

Dodge shook his head. "No, you'll best leave after *chores*. It wouldn't be decent of you to saddle me with all the haying."

"No, I don't guess it would." I smiled. "Sorry."

He nodded. "No sorry needed. Half of you ought to be spirit, and whenever you moon about that young lady, your heart should rightly foam and bubble like a bucket of fresh milk that's still under a cow." He smiled. "When y'all get here, we just might hold a celebration."

"A party?"

"I've done a lot dumber things," said Dodge. Then his face turned sober. "But right now, let's you and me quiet down, or we'll be owning a lot of dead horsemeat. That wild band'll keep circling in there until they drop. He already lost a few mares by pushing them too hard."

"You mean some of them *died?*"

"Son, horses do die, same as everybody else. Two days ago, I'd guess that stud had a mare or two more than right now. But don't fret on it, because it's Nature's way."

Thinking on it, I figured Dodge was right. Weaker trees fall, turn into soil, and resweeten the earth for a fresh seed.

"Well," said Dodge, moving away from the cordon, "our band won't enjoy a lick of repose if we stand here all night molesting 'em." Turning his back to the horses, he walked away. "We'll leave be until sunup."

"Dodge," I asked, "how come the mares went so willing inside the corral, just the way we wanted them to do?"

"Oh, I s'pose because they had stopped here before and found it a natural shelter, which in a way it is, overgrown and all. To them, it was home. Some of the olden horses probable even lay down in there to sleep, and have for a passable number of years. We were mighty fortunate I remembered this place existed."

We walked together.

"You and my father used to camp here, or so you said."

Dodge nodded. "The three of us, sometimes. Short Callum came along too, when he wasn't coon-dogging after the ladies."

I stopped.

"Where did my father sleep?"

Dodge studied me. "Is that important?"

"Yes."

"How come?"

"Because," I said, "if it's all the same to you, I'd sort of like to sleep on the same spot, just the way he did, so I can tell him about it when I get back home."

"Okay. That's important."

He walked toward the falling-down shed, which really was hardly more than a roof on stilts. "As I recollect," Dodge said, "Short and his dog, Lady Macbeth, usual slept underneath his horse, for warmth, until one night the horse was so tuckered out that he lay down too, on Short."

I laughed.

"Is that how he got so short?"

"No. I'd say Short was just intended to be a man of very average stature." He paused. "As for me, I'd sort of bunk anywhere, but your pa was fussy about sleep arrangements." Dodge looked around the shed floor which was nothing more than Florida sand. Then he pointed. "Over there. Right in that corner. Golly, I can picture Sam Bodeen now, curled up in a nook, snoring so hard that he'd disturb Satan."

I dragged my saddle to the place that Dodge had indicated. "Right here?"

He nodded. "You're on it."

"I just wanted to be closer to him," I told Dodge. "And it means something, because I know I can bring him back somehow. Not back to this place but back to the Buckle Tee. His body's been there all along, but his mind's been away since my mother was killed. It's not right, Dodge. It just isn't."

"I understand, boy."

"Thanks."

"Go to sleep. You and I had ourselfs a full day and a night longer. So flatten down and rope a Z. If my guess is a bull's-eye, your tomorrow is going to come up like golden music."

Grinning, I said, "Thanks, partner."

I lay down, hoping I could dream about how my father had slept here, hunting horses with Dodge and Short, in the old days. But my dreams turned out different. Somebody new to my life came to my dreams. Yet I was not intending to jump into a marriage. She had made the mistake of jumping too soon. Rolling over, I could picture her face, strong and honest, and I whispered her name.

"Cora."

# CHAPTER
## 26

DODGE TARRIED AT THE CORDON.

But after chores, I rode out pronto on my bay mare, Brownie, leading the saddled palomino, one of the two mares belonging to the D-bar-Y and so branded. It was a short ride, especially at the speed I was traveling, and I arrived to a whoa at Cora's shack about straight-up noon.

"Cora! It's me, Bad Bodeen."

Hearing, she dashed out of the shack just as I dismounted, ran to me, and then hugged the breath out of me. And it was certain very pleasant, feeling her sweet face pressed close to mine.

"Oh, Bad Bodeen," she said, as though saying it gave her pleasings. "I was afeared you'd never come back."

"But I told you so. I'd promised."

Looking me in the eyes, she said, "Yes, I recall you did, and honest, so I should've knowed you'd return."

"Where's Burlin?"

"Inside. He's asleep."

"Well, fetch him and let's go. You know you can't stay here and fend for a baby forever."

"Go where?"

"I found Dodge, and the two of us captured a band of wild horses, including the stallion, and we're having a celebration. You and Burlin are invited."

"Fine," she said. "I'll be ready by the time you can hook a leg over that there precious mare of yours."

She was. I don't guess I'd ever been a witness to anybody who could get herself ready to attend a celebration any quicker than Cora Blike. It seemed less than a minute. Out of the shack she exploded, carrying Burlin in one arm and a very large bundle of belongings over her opposite shoulder. She didn't bother to bring her worthless old shotgun.

Turning around, she looked at the shack.

"Good-bye," she said.

"What's all that stuff for?"

"I'm leaving this old place and coming with you." She paused. "If you want me to."

I smiled. "I want you to."

Cora sighed with a wide smile. Handing me the bundle, she mounted the palomino, then reclaimed her giant wad of possessions. "This, and Burlin, is all I got in the world," she said.

"No, it isn't," I said. "You got me for a friend."

She laughed. "And you got me, Bad Bodeen." We kissed this time like friends. "What day's today? Because I always aim to remember it forever."

I counted from the Kickaloo Junior Rodeo, which followed the Fourth of July, until now. "It's the tenth day of July," I said. Then it hit me. "Holy smoke, Cora. This is my birthday! I'm sixteen years old."

"Happy birthday," she said. "Now, let's get a wiggle on, before you collapse of old age." As we rode away, Cora looked one time over her shoulder at the shack where she had been living and raising her infant son. "Well, so much for that golden palace.

I couldn't have lasted there much longer. And now I'm so happy I could outjump a grasshopper."

"Just don't drop Burlin," I warned her.

"Never. I don't drop good people."

"Neither do I. Ever since I left you, I knew I'd be back to help you and Burlin along for a while. We live in a good-sized house, in Kickaloo, so there's room aplenty for you and your child."

Her face brightened. "I'd like that a lot. Besides, I know a way around that swamp where you lost a mule."

For a while, we rode along without saying too much. Burlin did all the talking, making his little baby noises whenever he was of a mind, which was often. He sounded a lot like music.

"How's Dodge?" Cora asked me.

"Oh, he's right dandy. And he sure knows how to hunt horses. Wait'll you see the string we caught, Cora. You won't believe it. We got back the three mares we lost, plus four other mares and the jackpot. A beauty of a white stallion."

Soon she said, "How much farther? I like being alone with you, Ladd, but I'm also hankering to see Mr. Dodge."

"Not much farther. Maybe a mile or two. Or three."

Cora sighed. "There sure is a lot of Florida."

"Agreed," I said. "A teacher at school, Miss Atherton, says that someday Florida will be one of the most populated states in all of America, soon as people discover how fair Florida is, and she says she hopes she's not alive to see the rush."

Cora glanced at me. "Do you go to *school?*"

"Not regular. How about you?"

"I almost finished the eighth," Cora said, "but Burlin up and finished me first."

The way she said it made me laugh. "Maybe," I told her, "we both ought to get more schooling. And for certain, soon as Burlin's old enough, he'd best store some learning."

"I s'pose so," Cora said. "Trouble is, if Burlin prospers smart on too many books, he'll realize that his ma don't know enough to boil beans."

"No he won't. Because you have natural brains, Cora. You know how to deal with difficulties and come up swinging . . . like how to spread blankets over an anthill. Now that's what I call practical."

"Thanks," she said, her chin in the air. "It sure is nifty to know that I can outsmart a louse."

We both had to laugh at that remark, and even little Burlin laughed some too.

Right soon, we arrived back at the corral. As we rode in, Dodge waved to the three of us. He was standing near the corral fence, talking to the stallion, but he left to join us as we were about to dismount. I was surprised when he reached up and took Burlin from Cora's hands, handling the little fellow in a comfortable manner. Come to think, it didn't amaze me that much, because Dodge Yardell had an easy way of tending things that were young, green, and growing.

Burlin started up a fuss.

So Dodge bounced Burlin gently on his shoulder. "There, there, there," he said in an extra-soft voice, "now let's don't carry on around Grampa Dodge thataway. Or else we'll just have to feed you to that big stallion over yonder, and he'll maybe suppose you're nothing more than a carrot, and eat you right up." He looked at me. "I'll mind the child for a while, so you can show our horses to Miss Cora."

When we were alone, Cora said, "Now that's how I'll expect you to grow up and be like. I hope you'll favor Dodge and be a southern gentleman the way he is. You already are in lots of ways, and this is one of the reasons I'm so partial on you."

"Cora," I said, "thanks, but I don't intend to grow up to be anybody except me . . . Ladd Bodeen."

She nodded her head once. "That is fair enough for me."

"All right," I told her. "Now we've got that matter settled, let's go look at our horses."

In daylight, the wild horses didn't look very prospering. Their manes had never been brushed, and the neck hair hung in sweat-twisted halyards. Some of their hoofs didn't look too healthy and one of the mares walked a step lame.

"The white is the stud. He's going to belong to Dodge because he wants him. It took him a few tries to cough it out, but he wants the stud, for keepers."

"Are you keeping the wild mares?"

"Well, maybe one. I'll sell the remainder to Mr. Jim Bob Grading, who owns a rodeo in Kickaloo."

Cora studied the horses for a minute or so, and then asked me, "Which mare'll you keep?"

"Well, maybe one that swells up and appears ready to drop a foal. The rest I'll sell to the rodeo. Our ranch usual has a few bills to pay, so the cash can ease up the pinch." I thought for a long moment. "Before selling off a single animal, however, I want my father to see the horses I'm bringing home. And to see his friend Dodge. Maybe all of it can help him get well in his head."

"Tell me about it," she said softly.

I nodded. "Sometime." My face had hardened, not for myself but for my father, but now it was softening, almost tempted to smile, because today was a special day. My birthday. The date wasn't so important. What mattered was the things I was doing. A few of them were personal. Not all. Much of it was for my family and my new friends. What tickled me the most was that nothing I was doing would be used to parade by Sue Louise

Hartberry, or Bill Tarky, or anyone in the town of Kickaloo
. . . and that even includes Mr. Jim Bob Grading. "Cora," I said,
"enjoy yourself a look at the horses for a minute or so. I'll be
right back."

I found Dodge.

He was sitting on a fallen tree, gently bouncing little Burlin
up and down on his knee, like a horse, and singing to him.

"Dodge, today's my birthday."

He smiled. "Well, best wishes."

"What's important is the fact that, for the first time in my life,
I'm starting to feel that maybe this boy might make it clear to
manhood."

Dodge nodded. "I'd wager so."

There was enough length of log for me to sit down too, so
I did, about six feet from Dodge and Burlin.

"Becoming a man isn't something that I'm doing all alone.
Several of you good people gave me a boost. Folks here, and back
home. That even includes my brother, who didn't intend to help,
yet he did. Right now I know Tate better than he knows me.
Better than he knows himself. He'll know me sudden soon. I'm
only sixteen. But inside I'm growing taller."

Still holding the baby, Dodge stood up. So did I. He looked
me straight in the face, as though taking a measurement. With
one little nod of his head, Dodge said, "A bit more than taller."

"Thanks."

With his free hand, Dodge reached out and smacked a punch
to my shoulder. Not hard.

It felt good.

# CHAPTER
## 27

DODGE PUT ON A FRESH SHIRT.

That same afternoon, he tossed a saddle on his chestnut Morgan, a horse he claimed was one hurrying bitch of an animal that could outrun Satan and then vault over Hell, and he rode off ahead of dust, at an easy gallop.

Earlier, as he was cinching the tack on his Morgan, I'd asked, "How come you're not taking the rib-counter buckskin?"

"The mare's fresher," he said, "and faster."

He was gone almost four hours. By the time he returned, it was after sundown, but Dodge Yardell was smiling.

"Where in heck have you been to?" I asked him. "Not that it's my business. It isn't."

"Oh, only over to Confederation."

"What's there?"

"A lady friend." He dismounted, holding a white square box that was tied three ways with string. He also had a few other packages in his saddlebags. "Here," he said, handing his mysterious white box to Cora. "I'd be obliged, Miss Cora, if you'd mind to care for this until after we eat."

As it turned out, the packages in his saddlebags contained our supper. Warm chicken, some fresh biscuits with honey to top them, and some cabbage slaw. Dodge also brought a big bag of raw carrots for the horses, and a small sack of oats. One by one, he handed these items to Cora Blike, almost as if the two of them lived there alone, and I wasn't around.

He shot Cora a wink.

"Please do it," he said.

Nary another word passed between the pair of them, and it certain made me begin to wonder exactly what was happening. Also, it seemed near a century since I'd been home at the Buckle Tee, and I would have traded off a lung, two ribs, and a kidney just to see Mrs. Skagg standing at our cookstove, in our kitchen, and serving me up a hot home-cooked meal.

"Chow's on," Cora told us.

Even though we ate on the ground, as usual, our supper was really good. By now, Dodge and I were both a mite ill of each other's cooking, so to taste the delights of Confederation's bounty was a welcome relief. We ate on paper plates. And we also had paper napkins to wipe the chicken grease off our chins. But every bite was so tasty that the paper wasn't even considered.

"Wow," I said. "This is food."

Cora ate like any minute it all was about to disappear, and she was right. Watching her made me wince, wondering how many times she had been hungry, and at the same time had given her breast to her empty child.

"Okay," said Dodge, "now the box."

Cora opened it.

Inside was a birthday cake. It was white with white icing, and a ring of angels on the frosting, all of them dancing around a ring that held the numerals 16.

"Happy birthday, Laddy," Dodge said. "In a way, you and I

are both sixteen, on account I'm sixty-one. And I been sixty-one now for at least five years. Maybe ten."

Cora kissed me, in a sisterly way.

Dodge spanked me. And hard!

Later on, Burlin woke up from his nap and joined our party to make us a foursome.

"Only a few days ago," Dodge said, as the four of us sat on the ground at a fire that was becoming smaller, "you were a boy astride a wooden merry-go-round pony."

I felt my chest puffing, inflated and fluffed up like a romantic cock pigeon. Well, I warned myself, let all this sweetsop go to your heart and not your head.

"Speech," ordered Dodge.

"Thank you both," I said. "In my whole life, I don't guess I ever had a birthday as happy as mine tonight. Inside, I got feelings for both of you people. So soak that in your ears and we'll call it even. Okay?"

Dodge said, "Amen."

For several minutes, nobody said much of anything, with the exception of Burlin, who let out a coo, sounding happier than a nested dove.

"Now then," Dodge final said, "we got some sleeping plans to solve." He looked fierce to me, then at Cora, and I knew right then that he wasn't planning for me to enjoy another birthday present that might make a baby. It was fine with me. Even though I already knew, obviously, that Cora Blike had made a baby with somebody, it would be a question that would remain buried, a forever secret.

In my heart, however, I'd been hoping to be able to sleep *near* Cora, the way we had before on the night the rain had fallen so hard.

Yet the expression on Dodge Yardell's face warned me that I'd best put forward my finest manners, and enjoy the pleasurings that were available, ignoring those beyond reach. It was more than a boyhood feeling. More than being a kid, and far more than anything I'd ever felt for Sue Louise Hartberry.

"Tomorrow," said Dodge, "maybe it ought to be right for you three people to head north to the Buckle Tee."

I looked at him in disappointment. "You're not coming?"

"Yes." He grinned. "I'll be along. But perhaps it'll require me a day or so with the stallion. Just the pair of us. Laddy, you take the mares. All four. One or two are maybe settled pregnant and will drop foals before too long. As for myself, all I want is to be alone with the stud, the pair of us. Two old warriors. We'll get along right handsome."

I nodded. "Yes, you probable ought." But there was something else on his mind, I felt.

However, on the following morning, Dodge was about to let me push a band of mares and geldings north, toward Kickaloo.

"Now," he told me, "the best thing to remember is this, Laddy. You got a young mother and a baby along, so there's no need to drive hard. Take it lazy. The important matter is to get home with your charges. Now, just in case I never make it, I'll be hoping you keep some of the mares until they either foal or don't. When they drop, and if one's a colt, keep him *male*. Don't cut him. Hear?"

"I hear." In my mind, what Dodge was saying was about to worry me serious.

"He'll make your Buckle Tee outfit a fine stallion," Dodge said. "Trust me on this. I know horses like I know my own soul."

"How quick will you be along?" I asked him.

"Sudden soon. You can count on my intentions. I got me a hanker to visit Sam Bodeen."

"Before we leave," Cora said to Dodge, as though she was as

concerned as I was, "I'd consider it a righteous honor if you'd be a godfather to my baby. Would you?"

Dodge nodded. "I'd be pleased."

"You see," Cora told us, "Burlin ain't never been baptized, and it weighs heavy on my worrying. So, let's do a few drops of water on him, and say words above him, to make it all legal and proper."

We did it.

"I never been baptized," said Dodge. "Have you?"

"No," I said, "I don't guess so."

"And me neither," Cora admitted. "So that makes Burlin the luckiest one amongst us."

I mounted my bay, Brownie.

Dodge Yardell decided that his palomino mare would be the most gentle mount for Cora, seeing that she also had to hold Burlin along the way.

All the other horses, except for the white stallion, would be coming with us, collected. We also would be taking both saddles, at Dodge's insistence, because he said that he'd not need one, providing circumstances proved to his liking.

I stared at him. "You aren't intending to ride north, bareback, on that white hellion. Are you?"

Before answering, Dodge glanced over at the cordon. "We'll maybe learn," he said, "if I can claim myself a horseman, or not."

Again I looked at him, this time for about near a minute. "No," I final told him, "you aren't going to do it, on account it's my responsibility, this trip to the Buckle Tee, so I'm taking charge."

"What are you saying, boy?"

"Please listen up," I said. "You're well over sixty-one years old, and that's too dang close to busting all your brittle old bones, trying once more to crow about what a tough old rooster you used to be."

For a minute, nobody spoke.

"Just what do you mean?" he asked. "Spit it out."

I hauled in a deep breath.

"Eight seconds," I told him.

His face became a question. "What exactly are you talking to me about?"

"This time," I said, "my brother won't be here to see it, regardless of whether I fall or stick. But I've made up my mind, Dodge. You and Cora and the baby are riding ahead to the Buckle Tee. The stallion and I will be following."

"Are you loco?"

"Possible so," I told him.

Dodge cuffed back his Stetson, a gesture that I had by now concluded was an indication of his doubt. "You're still a boy, Laddy. Nobody expects you to fork some unbroke wild stallion and train him for riding even if he's near to being thirty. Maybe more. As far as I know, nobody's ever attempted such, so why should you? There's no need for you to prove yourself so hard."

I took a deep breath. "Yes," I said, "there truly is. Not to Tate or you or Cora, or even to my father. It'll be between that stallion in there and me. The way I figure it, every day the stud is aging, and every day I'm growing. It's what I aim to do, Dodge, so don't waste air trying to change my mind."

Dodge was quiet for a spell. So was Cora. They looked at each other and then back at me.

During this time, I was busy with my own thoughts, not theirs. In a way, it was sort of a shame to deprive Dodge of the chance to ride the stallion. Yet, even though he would have hated to admit it, the old man maybe needed some protection. However, the thought that Dodge would sometime be riding his white prize home, with a saddle, all the way south to his ranch, pleased me. But that would be the proper time for the two of them. Instead of now.

"All right," Dodge told me, "we'll cut a bargain. I'll let you try to ride the stallion. But soon as he bucks you off the first time, let's call it square and you'll quit. And I'll take over." He held out his right hand. "Deal?"

We shook.

"Deal."

# CHAPTER
## 28

WE WAITED TWO MORE DAYS.

During that time, Dodge cut down a deer with the Remington. It was a young forkhorn and we ate well. We fed the horses hay. The mares ate, but for three days I'd not seen the stallion eat even one mouthful of cut grass, or sleep. Due to his age he began to tire. Even before we caught the wild horses they were already pushed hard.

Our plan was slowly working. A gentling plan.

"King," said Cora. "That ought to be your new stallion's name, because he certain is one."

Dodge and I agreed. The name, which Dodge had also used, stuck. King.

"Today," I told them, "I'm feeling lucky, and I'd like to slap a saddle on that old fellow. That is, if it's okay with you, Dodge. He's your animal."

Dodge didn't answer.

Cora did. She was holding Burlin, yet she moved closer to where I was standing outside the corral fence. "Please take careful, Bad Bodeen," she told me. "I'm not fixing to lose a friend like you so early."

"You won't lose me, Cora," I said. "I've ridden broncs before." I didn't tell her how unsuccessfully.

I looked at the massive white stallion. I'd already decided that, if I did manage to stick on him, I wouldn't bother to tell Tate about it. Doing the job would be ample enough. Bragging would be excess frosting. Besides, upon my returning to the Buckle Tee with my parade of fresh acquirings, Tate would see for himself that I hadn't been idle. He'd ask about the missing mule, which I still felt bad about, but then I could show him the fresh brands on four mustang mares, a new **BT** on each one.

Today, however, could be raw going.

"Eight seconds," I said quietly, recalling the black Galloway bull.

This time, I knew, eight seconds wouldn't cut it, not by a long shot. It would be more liken to a minute before King would accept me as a rider, a man who could *stick*. It was strange, but I sort of had a hunch that I might be able to do it, even though King was an unrode stallion. In a sense, nobody would be watching, because this had to be a showdown between man and animal, between Ladd Bodeen and King, a wild unbroken stud of Republic Flat.

A year ago, I'd made a fair bronc ride at the Kickaloo Junior Rodeo, so I had a little experience under my belt. My buckleless belt. Never had I stuck all the way to the buzzer. When would the buzzer sound here—or would it?

Dodge looked at the stallion, then at me. "Laddy," he said in his quiet voice, "it won't be like sitting on one of my wooden carousel ponies. So I hope you realize what a trip it'll be on that cusser."

I nodded.

The old gentleman sighed. "For sure, I pray you're not doing this to show off for Miss Cora. It's not needed. She already looks at you like you're the biggest orange on the tree."

I grinned. "Thanks. I'm not doing it to show off."

"Not even a little?"

To tell you the straight of it, Dodge Yardell, I wanted to say, I'm doing it because if I don't, some nice old man will probable try it and maybe hurt himself. But I didn't say my thoughts aloud to Dodge. After all, I couldn't wash away his pride and tell him that, good as he was, he was too old to saddle-break this white hurricane.

We tossed a loop on him.

For the better part of an hour, King fought the rope around his neck, but then Dodge worked the tiring animal into circling a trot, around and around inside the cordon. He then told me to fetch a pad and saddle. Then, while Cora held the distant end of the rope, Dodge and I blindfolded King and put a saddle on his back, gently, and cinched it tight.

Mounted on his Morgan mare, Dodge did most of the crowding, forcing the stallion to walk a circle between his mare and the fence. Around and around. The stallion was tired, hungry, and a lot of the fight seemed to have left him. Circle by circle, King was getting used to the weight of a saddle on his spine. My weight, however, would be a hotter heft.

Finally the stallion stopped.

"We're ready," Dodge told me.

"Okay," I said, "but I'm going to ask a favor of you."

"What's that?"

"When I mount him, and before you remove his blindfold, I want you to link my feet together, under his belly."

"No." Dodge shook his head. "Son, that's a fooly thing to do. Because if that stallion decides to roll on you, you'll be crushed to a pulp. And you'll never give your sweet Miss Cora another kiss, or anything else."

"Do it anyways," I said. "I'll chance it. It'll help my legs to clamp around him solid."

Dodge scratched his face. "Well, maybe we can compromise. I'll link the stirrups together under his belly, and it'll afford you a tighter seat, yet it won't trap you if he's rolling. Agreed?"

"Agreed," I said.

Dodge mashed a carrot and smeared the orange pulp on a rope halter that he'd woven in only a minute's time. He slipped it on the head of the blindfolded stud easier than I thought was possible, then looked me in the eye. Now, when he spoke, his voice was harder than cold iron. "You about ready to visit Hell?"

"I'm ready."

Somewhere, in my memory, I could hear the five-piece band at the Kickaloo Junior Rodeo, smell the arena's dung-infested sawdust, and hear the announcer's bullhorn. "Folks . . . it's a youngster from the Buckle Tee ranch, coming out of chute number one on a white mustang stallion that ain't never before been rode, or even mounted. Laddy Bodeen . . . on *King*."

I was up on the top rail of the fence now. Cora was outside, holding Burlin.

"Do it," she said, "because you're Bad Bodeen."

Dodge was on his mare, and he would stay mounted and inside the corral, out of harm's way, during my ride. Yet, if he spotted trouble, he could get to me quick and snake me off. If I got tossed, he could at least ride between me and the stud, so I wouldn't be too badly stomped.

As I let myself down easy on the saddle and grabbed the two rope reins with both hands, I could feel King's body trembling. Maybe it was my body too. Please, I told myself, do not throw up.

I pulled my hat down tight.

Dodge winked at me. And then he said his final word. Only one, but I liked how it sounded. It hit me like a nail.

"*Stick,*" he said.

"Yank it off," I answered, "and turn him loose."

With a real easy gesture, Dodge removed the stud's blindfold, backed his mare away, and suddenly the two of us were alone. King and me.

I felt his body crouch as he gathered himself underneath my weight, his hindquarters digging in for about a second. Then, with one forceful spring, he was in the air, and the band was playing. As he landed, the saddle rammed me like it was made out of oak, kicking me between my legs. It hurt bad. Right then, I fought the first urge to chicken off, knowing I wouldn't. I couldn't quit. This was more than just another try on Crankshaft, paid for by my brother.

I'd guessed that the old stallion had been weakened by fatigue, lack of rest, and very little food . . . but I had guessed wrong. His body was now all power, fighting male power that resented the unfamiliar man and weight on his back. He bucked clear across the enclosure, turned, and bucked all the way back. In midair he'd twist his body, shaking, kicking, pitching, snorting his venom at the world. I didn't have to keep one arm in the air for rodeo points, or kick my boots forward so that my heels would rake his shoulders. My feet were tightly contained at his ribs, stirrup bound.

As soon as I could, for every one of King's bucks, I relaxed my body to sway and absorb the jolting shocks, moving as he moved, giving him all the freedom he could muster.

I was sticking.

But the stallion wouldn't quit. And right then I knew what old Dodge had meant about a visit to Hell. I was there.

Again and again he left the ground, only to return to it with a thudding impact that pounded me with pain. My backbone repeatedly snapped like a whip. How I held on I couldn't understand, but I *stuck*. As the stud's head was shaking so violently, my fingers lost one of the rope reins. Lashing free, it cut me across the face, and I somehow grabbed it again. The stud tried to wipe me off against the inside of the fence, but I managed to rein him toward the center of the corral.

I couldn't see Dodge or his mare, as though both had vanished. Nor could I see Cora. Much of the time I couldn't see the stallion I was riding. My eyes kept closing to fight off the dust and the grit that was being kicked up by four flying hoofs.

When the stallion fell, crashing down on his side, I was quick enough to extract my under leg until the animal could regain his feet. All this happened in about two seconds. Had my boots been roped together, my leg would have been smashed, along with a few other necessities. As the stallion rose to his feet, I stayed in the saddle.

Now I couldn't kick my free boot into the stirrup, but final did.

The stallion was breathing hard, panting, each breath he took was labor and dust and exhaustion. His and mine.

Then, for a moment, he quit bucking and stood shaking in the center of the corral, his sweaty body frosted with dirt. Dodge trotted his mare around in circles and I was preparing myself for the stallion's next attack.

It never came.

"Gather him in, boy. And he's yours."

I did what Dodge advised.

"All right, now walk him in a circle." Dodge was riding beside me now, and I could feel his knee bump mine. "Collect him, but keep him moving with your heels at his ribs. Hold him under you, in your command." Reaching out a hand, Dodge stroked the stud's neck. "You done proud, old fellow. There's nothing in you to be ashamed of. Besides, you've earned yourself some new friends, and some new mares too."

Leaning over, he fed his new stallion a carrot. It wasn't eaten right away, only rejected, then sniffed at, and slowly accepted with a decidedly hungry munch.

I hurt so much that I couldn't talk, and could only stammer. "Did . . . I . . . stick?"

Dodge patted my back. "In all my days as a Florida horse man, I don't guess nobody ever put on a better show. Good ride. Ladd, I'm doggone glad to know you."

His words made me swallow. More than once. My anus was on fire and my privates felt as though they'd been ground up for sausage, but despite the hurting, I felt hard and healing. I'd stuck. Both the stallion and I gave it every ounce. The feeling was a notch higher than a belt buckle.

I'd rode a king, and felt like a prince.

# CHAPTER
## 29

WE HEADED NORTH.

As we rode through the little town of Confederation, about a dozen or so people stared at us, their mouths gaping, as though we were a traveling freak show.

From their point of view, I'll have to admit, we must have created a rather peculiar parade: an old gentleman, a boy of sixteen, a very young girl breasting a baby, two geldings, seven mares, and a battle-scarred and unbranded stallion named King. For the citizens of Confederation, our passing through was hardly the type of event viewed every day. Or every decade. Their mouths were as popped open as their eyes.

We stopped briefly in the town to trade for a few supplies, mostly food, carrots and oats for ten horses, and then we continued north.

Dodge chuckled. "Did you get a look at their faces? Like they'd seen a herd of spooks in broad daylight." He laughed again and slapped his thigh.

I'll give credit to Dodge. He honest enough took his turn carrying the baby, so Cora and I could walk along by our lonesomes, holding hands. For a spell, I couldn't figure out how

Dodge had learned to be so useful at baby-tending, but then concluded that he was the measure of a gentleman who could do about anything he set a purchase on, with babies or people or horses. Maybe I'd try to be like him.

On the way north, thanks to what Cora knew, and Dodge too, we didn't go near the swamp where the gator had killed Evelyn, my mule. We went around it, even though it was ten miles to the east, then north again.

One by one, landmarks began to appear familiar to me. For example, a water tower. And it was a joyous feeling to know that by tomorrow sometime, I'd be nearing home and everybody at the Buckle Tee.

I'd be seeing Papa.

Also it was Tate Bodeen that I couldn't wait to witness. Oh, I'd be happy enough to see Gusher, Slim, and to hug Mrs. Skagg. Yet, as I rode along on my bay mare, it was my brother's face that kept appearing in my imagining: Tate's jaw, and those steely eyes. I had no intention of telling Tate a doggone thing. Instead, he could stare at all of us, our entire menagerie, and then choke himself crazy on his own questions.

It made me laugh aloud.

Cora looked at me. "What's funny, lamb?"

"Oh," I said, "it could possible be my brother, who right now doesn't yet know how amusing he's about to become."

"You don't wrongly hate your brother, do you? If you admit so, I don't guess I'd most believe it. You couldn't hate a soul. Hate's not inside you."

"No, I don't hate my brother."

Our hands met, and squeezed.

"I'm some fearful," Cora said. "Maybe all those family folks of yours won't want Burlin or me to stay on there, even for a week."

"All that matters," I told her, "is that I want you to stay, and so be it. You'll be a guest on *my* half of the Buckle Tee, not on Tate's. You and Burlin couldn't stay in that shack. So somebody had to do something to move you out."

Nothing was said for a mile or more.

"Look at that," Cora said.

Behind us, Dodge was riding his Morgan with his right leg hooked around the saddle horn, so that both his boots were on the left flank of his horse. In his lap he was holding Burlin and singing to him. "Oh Genevieve, sweet Genevieve . . ."

"If Burlin had hatched out a girl," Cora said, "I reckon I'd had to call her Genevieve, or else."

We took turns riding, walking, holding Burlin, and keeping all our horse stock together so they wouldn't scatter all over Florida. The mares stayed ahead of King. He somehow had accepted us, perhaps due to being tired or old, plus the fact that Dodge guessed that nobody before us had ever given King a carrot. And it was carrots he adored like candy. Right now, King seemed even more tired than Dodge.

"Brother," said Dodge, "soon's we all git somewhere, to Heaven or Hell or to the Buckle Tee, I'm about fixing to grab sleep until winter." He laughed. "It's been a spell since I done so much work on so dang little pay."

Cora smiled. "Ain't he a dreadful wonder?"

"Yes," I said, "he certain is."

To look at him, I felt proud that my daddy, Sam Bodeen, had selected a man like Dodge Yardell to be his saddle buddy. It would have been enjoyable to have seen Short and Dodge and Sam herding a bunch of cattle, or as three horse hunters. Florida was changing. Perhaps there wouldn't be any more mustangs. I promised to ask our library teacher, Miss Atherton, about that, because she'd certain know. She was like Dodge, or Cora, and knew a lot of useful stuff.

It hit me!

Miss Atherton's first name was . . . Genevieve.

Yes, it was Genevieve Atherton. That I knew for sure, and maybe when we got home I'd ask Dodge if he'd cotton to make the acquaintance of a nice lady that I liked a whole lot, even if she was a schoolteacher.

Nobody's perfect.

This realization sort of reminded me of something that Cora had told me, when we'd first met, about people and perfection. "The Lord," Cora had said, "doesn't bake perfect people like cookies on a sheet."

Although I couldn't exact explain why, or how, just cogitating on the way Cora Blike said her piece helped me to understand people like Tate and my father. Never would I expect them to be faultless because we Bodeens don't hatch that way. At my last rodeo, a bull showed all the local people that I couldn't touch perfect for even eight seconds.

Gusher didn't care.

He would've still been dear old Gusher Plant even if'n I'd got tossed off a hundred times. A thousand times. Mrs. Skagg didn't care either. I'd come to realize that such people were all pure gold. Maybe not the pure part. For certain, gold. As I rode along, progressing north toward the town of Kickaloo, I was deciding about a whole passel of things, to enrich my future. Maybe my life would be half Cora. And the other half would be the Buckle Tee. Whatever, it'd be home.

Cora was busy nursing Burlin.

So as not to trespass on her privacy, Dodge rode up along beside me, in front, and cranked up a conversation. "All right, son, you can tell me about Sam now, if you're of a mind."

I nodded. "It happened fourteen years ago, when I was about two. Papa insisted that he could break any horse so that a woman could ride it. So he made my mother ride an unruly red roan gelding, and it didn't work out."

"What happened?"

"The roan threw her and broke her neck. From all I know, my mother got instant killed, and then my father turned haywire and killed the roan. Then, after Mama's funeral, he retreated inside himself like he was hiding from all that had happened. When I was growing up, the only father I knew was a man who sat silent, with a little blanket over his knees."

Dodge shook his head. "That is so downright sad."

"That's not all. My brother, Tate, blamed Papa for the death of our mother, because he was only twelve years old at the time. These days he doesn't go near Papa at all. Instead he climbs the little rise behind our house and visits Mama's grave. He pats the earth with his hand, but if I'd dare mention it to him, Tate would probable bust his knuckles on me."

Dodge sighed. "Sounds to me like he's already busted, somewhere inside himself."

"Maybe so," I told Dodge. "All I know is that I'm glad I could tell you about the place and the people you'd soon be meeting in Kickaloo."

Dodge clucked to his mare. "And you, Laddy . . . you been toting all this load around on your shoulders, as though it was only yours to burden."

"No," I said, "because Tate's been carrying it too. He doesn't yet know that I understand."

Dodge was quiet for a time.

"Ladd," he said, as we rode north, "years back, I was stricken in love with a gal whose name was Lola May Tate. But she went off to marry somebody else. Your pa. At the time I was heart-broke. But the years ticked by and gentled me back to reason. So now you know why I never come north to visit y'all. I wasn't man enough to see Lola May as Mrs. Sam Bodeen."

I couldn't breathe for about a full minute. "You were in love with . . . my mother?"

Dodge nodded. "Yes, I'm honored to say that I was, and I'll never regret it. Never. She was my sweetheart."

I took a deep breath. "Then, if things had panned out different, you just might have been my pa." I swallowed. "Every time you called me *son,* I sort of wondered about that, because you seemed to be part of my family."

Dodge said nothing for a minute or two.

"To be honest about it," he admitted, "I sort of wish I had been your father. Maybe your life would've rode a sunnier trail."

"Maybe so," I told him. "But right now, my life's about to turn into all right, now that I've tackled a few jobs."

"Good," he said.

It was one of Dodge's favorite words, one that he used whenever he was pleased about the way matters were turning. Right about now, things were hatching out into sunshine. Like a warm summer morning.

"Soon," I told Dodge, "we'll be arriving at the Buckle Tee, and you'll be seeing Sam. He won't be alike to the pal whose company you and Short once enjoyed. It'll be another Sam Bodeen, a lot leaner than when the two of you were horse hunters."

Dodge sighed. "Yes, my lad, we were horse hunters, Sam and I. We rode together. It was oft times the three of us, Sam and me and Short Callum, and that infernal Lady Macbeth." Dodge shook his head. "What an unholy name for a dang dog." He chuckled. "At the time, Short was spooning with a gal whose name was Beth. As I recall, Beth Wallingford. And this doggone dog was living with 'em, and she would let loose her bowels on the rug. Not the lady, the dog. Although it amused Short, it certain did rankle this Miss Wallingford. And so Short, who got hisself drunk one evening, looked at the puddle on the carpet and said ... 'Out, out, dang spot.' Seems like it didn't amuse old Beth. With the help of a stove poker, she up and pounded the breathing out of Short and the dog, and then threw them outdoors into bad weather. And since then, Short Callum referred to his mongrel bitch as the Lady Macbeth."

"Why?" I asked.

Dodge sighed. "Dang if I know."

# CHAPTER
## 30

HOME.

There it was, wet from a fresh summer sun-shower, glistening and shining and ours.

Right then, deep inside me, I shared the feeling that my brother held in his heart for our little hunk of Florida. More than money, it was true wealth, like some gold and silver treasure, yet green.

Like a parade, we passed between the twin posts and underneath the weathered-gray arching sign with a **BT**. It was worth my salute. Slowly, we rode toward our house and barns, and my heart was pounding a happy tempo. "Home," I said. What a welcoming word. As we neared our outbuildings, Gusher was whitewashing the tack shed. The old man always claimed that a slap of whitewash could cover up everything except a Sunday-morning conscience.

I yelled to him. "Gusher, I'm back!"

Turning around, he spotted me, then went running toward the house, hollering, and waving his hat. Out of the kitchen door came Mrs. Skagg, hurriedly followed by Slim and slowly by Tate, on crutches.

"I reckon that handsome rascal is your brother," Cora said as we all rode closer.

"Handsome? He's not handsome at all," I said. *"I'm* the one that inherited all the noble features, not to mention personality."

We rode nearly to the dooryard. Me, Dodge, Cora, and the baby, plus two geldings (one of which was the skinny rib counter), seven mares, and an aging white warrior of a stallion. Dodge had tossed a loose loop around the stud's neck, just to keep him collected, but the old horse seemed to be willing enough to be with us. Carrots, oats, and caring had helped to docile him.

The expression on my brother's face was more entertaining than a rodeo and a circus added together. It was obvious that his busted ribs were still nagging him, and Tate was looking meaner than a sore tooth.

"Is he always so sour?" Cora whispered to me.

"No, not always. Sometimes he'll frown all day. Then, during supper, his face blooms to a scowl."

As the three of us dismounted, Cora holding her baby, the residents of the Buckle Tee couldn't quite seem to decide where to gape first, or what to ask next. Even old Gusher had dried up, a phenomenon that occurred with the frequency of Halley's comet. But then, as his face brightened, he extended a hand.

"Howdy," said Dodge.

"By the jingles," Gusher said, "if you ain't Dodge Yardell."

The two older men shook hands.

"Gusher Plant," said Dodge, "you sure got olden." He smiled. "But don't complain, Gush, because most people your age lie around in damp boxes."

"Yeah," said Gusher, "but your voice still sounds like every night you gargle with cream."

They both snorted a laugh.

Mrs. Skagg hugged me so hard I thought my aching ribs

would be worse off than Tate's. Then, releasing her hold, she inspected me up and down. "Nobody but you," she said, "could manage to get so dirty in little more than a week."

Gusher and Slim both pumped my hand and slapped my back. It felt welcoming. I was, however, waiting for my brother to tune up his growl, which he final got the gumption to do.

"Laddy," he said, as he eyed the ten horses and Cora *and the baby,* "would you mind telling us what in the name of Tarnation you've been doing?"

I bent him a grin. "Horse hunting."

Tate extended his hand to Dodge, who was standing closer to him than Cora was. But then Tate turned to her, again eyeing the baby, and said, "Yes'm, I'm Tate Bodeen. And it's my sorrowful lot in life to serve as Ladd's brother." He paused. "And who might you be?"

"Oh," I said quickly, "I didn't mean to neglect my company manners. Folks, allow me to present Miss Cora Blike and her baby, Burlin. Mr. Yardell, here, is the little boy's godfather, and I'm sort of his acting guardian. Cora, this lady is Mrs. Skagg. These gentlemen are Mr. Gusher Plant and Mr. Slim Service." They nodded. "And the poor soul on crutches cottons to brag that he's my busted horse-kicked brother, Tate."

Cora smiled. "Pleased to know y'all."

Before I knew it, Mrs. Skagg was holding and adoring Burlin, and he seemed to be enjoying the attention, cooing away. Then, as everyone was talking all to once, I near about split my face with smiling when Mrs. Skagg handed little Burlin to my brother to hold.

"How come you're giving the baby to me?" Tate asked, dropping both of his crutches and taking the bundle uneasily.

Mrs. Skagg laughed. "Because he's wet."

I near doubled over laughing.

"Well," said Mrs. Skagg, reclaiming Burlin away from Tate, "I just knew that my young Mr. Ladd would have himself an enterprise, and arrive home prospering. But I never suspected he'd return with Mr. Dodge Yardell, ten horses, a pretty girl, and a little cherub of a baby." She sighed. "It all must've been written in the stars."

"Stars?" Gusher chimed in. "I once got smitten sweet on the daughter of a genuine astrologist, and her father knew the Zodiac forwards, back, and sideways. All them stars and signs. But when he informed me that his daughter was a Virgo, I said *forget her fancy morals. Can she cook?*"

"Did you marry her?" Slim asked.

"Well, she went packing off to the city of Orlando to select a wedding dress, and stayed in a gussy hotel. Sent me a telegram saying that she had a room with Running Water, so I sent her a telegram back, telling her to keep going and to take the dang Seminole with her."

Dodge chuckled. "People never change. And neither do old jokes." But then his face turned sober. "Seems like there's maybe somebody missing here."

"Don't budge," Gusher said quickly. "I think Mr. Sam ought to come outside here and assay them new mustangs."

Gusher and Slim hurried to the house, then slowly returned, bringing Papa along between them. He was wearing his old bathrobe. My father said nothing as they approached, yet I noticed that his gaze was straight. Looking at Dodge Yardell, I could see that my new friend was surprised to see a Sam Bodeen that he'd never known. Half a Sam.

"He's . . . he's a pale shadow," Dodge sighed.

At last the two old horse hunters faced each other. Dodge stood alone, but Papa stood with the help of Gusher and Slim. Yet their eyes seemed to reach out for one another.

"Well," said Dodge, "it's good to notice ya, Sam." He pointed back over his shoulder. "Your son and I been hunting mustangs together, down to Republic Flat. As you can well see we managed to collect a few. In case you don't recognize me, my name's Dodge. You remember."

Right then, I was praying Papa would recall, as Dodge talked, because a person's voice is the last thing to change.

My father's mouth trembled.

Parting his lips, he stared open-mouthed at his longtime side-kick, and held the expression for about a minute. Then he spoke. "Where?" he said. "Where . . . is . . . Short?"

Dodge bit his lip. "Short's gone, Sam." The smooth voice became hoarse. "He's been clean gone more'n five years now. I was the only mourner to attend Short's funeral." Walking forward, Dodge put his arms gently around Papa and held him. "All I got now is you." Holding him close, Dodge touched his face and his white hair, patting his frail shoulder with a quieting hand. "Sam," he whispered, "do you remember?"

Papa nodded. "I remember, Dodge."

Watching, I was blaming myself for not preparing Dodge a bit more on how Papa would now appear. No longer the two-fisted Sam Bodeen. I read the shock on Dodge's face. Again he stroked the back of my daddy's head, the way a person would touch a good dog. "It's over, Sam," he said, his voice shaking. "You recollect that I had feelings about Lola May too, same as you, years ago. I lost her. Now we both lost her. We can't bring her back, and we can't bring back Short Callum." Dodge's voice was trembling. "All we best do is tend to the living."

Taking a step closer to Cora, I put my arm around her, to let her feel the strength of our protection. For some reason, Slim Service stood nearer to Gusher and to Mrs. Skagg, between them, as though they were the only parents he knew. Without crutches,

Tate limped to me, his eyes telling me that he'd seen what I had seen, as two old gentlemen held each other.

"Laddy," he said, "I don't guess that God made me strong enough to watch this. Looks like you brought us back a lot more than mustangs, brother." He rested a hard hand on my shoulder. "Maybe you brought us back Sam." He looked me in the eye. "Thank you, Ladd. You did what I could never do. You're a smack more than a bull rider."

As though ashamed, Tate put his arms around me, holding me to him with muscles like girders, arms that had chored seven days a week on the Buckle Tee since he'd been twelve, and scared to wonder if he could pull us all through, and make a go of it. I'd wager there had been countless nights when everyone else slept, but Tate lay awake and clenched a boy's fists, and prayed. I knew him better now than he could ever realize, and I liked him the way he was, because he was all Tate.

He was the Buckle Tee.

He was home.

As his face pressed hard against mine, I felt the stubble of his beard on my cheek, harsh, unyielding, so like the Tate we'd known. But now his cheeks were no longer dry, and he wasn't afraid to show it. Or share it. I was so much prouder to call him my brother. Eyes closed tight, I hugged Tate with everything in me, feeling him sob, and trying to heal him.

"I know, Tate. I know."

As I held him, all the years of hardness and hatred seemed to be emptying out of him, as though his long night of being alone had ended.

"I don't guess," he said, "I been much of a family to you, Laddy." He swallowed. "Can I try again?"

"Sure," I said. "Because you're going to try again for Papa." Looking over at Dodge and Sam holding to one another, I said,

"Tate, someday, with luck, we'll be two old gentlemen. Let's make us good times to save."

Tate nodded.

Releasing me, he pulled back to study me up and down. Then his face changed. It was a grin that he must have been holding prisoner inside his soul for thirteen years, because it blossomed like sunshine.

"Brother," he told me, "maybe we all came home."

ROBERT NEWTON PECK is the author of many books for adults and children. He has been a farmer, a soldier (machine gunner, 88th Infantry, World War II), a lumberjack, a football player, and a hog butcher.

His favorite fan letter is from a young reader who wrote: "Dear Rob . . . I like your books better than literature."